Disclaimer

This a work of fiction and fantasy, written for entertainment purposes *only*. It is NOT meant to be a how-to or expose of alternative lifestyles. Neither the author or publisher assume responsibility or liability if one attempts the practices or scenes found in this work.

Those that may be inclined to participate in alternative lifestyle activities are encouraged to seek out reputable instruction and information. The dictum of "Safe, Sane and Consensual" should always be followed.

Female Domination
Short Stories Volume I
Constance Pennington Smythe

Copyright © 2009
ISBN 978-1-934446-40-9
Cover Art and Illustrations
by Sardax

Published by
Romance Divine LLC
www.romancedivine.com

For My Lovely 'Gurls'

You Know Who You Are

A Special Thank You
To
Esteemed Artist
Sardax
For
His Wonderful Illustrations

Female Domination Short Stories
Volume I

Constance Pennington Smythe

Illustrations By Sardax

She picked up the phone and punched in a number. "Hello – I'm fine – I'm here with your big brother."

He grimaced; she was talking to Karen, his younger sister – step sister – who'd always been a pain for him.

"Of course he's gagged, who'd be interested in hearing anything he has to say – the inflatable one, he hates it – I don't know, I'll ask."

She grabbed his leash and jerked on it, pulling his head up. "Baby sister wants me to give the gag a couple of pumps, in her honor. You don't mind do you?"

Cuckold Date

He hated the rubber gag. Hated the way it tasted. Hated the way it made him drool. Most of all he hated the way it filled him, pushing his tongue to the bottom of his mouth and filling his cheeks so he looked like some version of a feminized and sissified Dizzy Gillespe.

She held the rubber pump ball in her hand, her fingers lightly curled over it. Her creamy skin and blood-red nails provided a stark contrast to the black, mottled surface of the ball. She slightly tugged the hose to his gag pulling his head forward. This close to her he smelled the fragrance of her bath soap, took in the hint of her perfume from the labored breathing through his nose.

"Too tight?" she mocked in her sing-song voice. It was meant to be pleasing and girly, but nothing she did would ever hide the menacing derision in her tone. Their innocent sex games had long ago taken a wicked turn that brought them to this point; Dominant Evil Mistress and submissive sissy maid. Tonight's celebration would mark another relationship milestone: CUCKOLD.

The fingers of her free hand found his nipple and gave it a vicious pinch. "I asked if it was too tight!" The melodious voice was gone, replaced by one evoking terror.

He never knew how to answer. There was NEVER a right answer, she would twist and turn his responses, always taking him where SHE wanted to go. He shook his head *no*, his eyes telling her that the gag wasn't too tight, that he would bear the discomfort - for HER.

It was exactly the response she'd wanted, although she always made him pay, and dearly, no matter what the response. "No?" the sing-song voice returned. "Then let's give it a couple more pumps…shall we?" She cocked her head, her eyes narrowing and her lips forming a thin, cruel smile. She loved this moment, when the realization set in, when he realized the trap had been set and shut, when his eyes pleaded with her, for mercy, for compassion. *Sorry, baby, not today, time to suffer.*

She squeezed the ball violently, the veins in her hand rising as she clamped down. The whisper of air down the tube was followed by his moans as the gag expanded. His eyes went wide and his "mmpphh, mmp-phh" noises brought a chuckle to her lips. "Darling, I can't understand a word you're saying." The second squeeze made his eyes water.

A perfectly manicured finger wiped away a tear and rubbed on the tip of his nose. "Yes, I believe that's better." Her hand grazed his swollen cheeks, the fingers slowly tracing over the skin stretched so tight, "Perhaps a bit of color on those puffy little cheeks." She took a brush and some blush from her dressing table, "A bit of color for my sissy slut." When she finished, his cheeks were beautifully rendered with a peach blush, further enhancing their enormous size.

With a quick tug on his leash she pulled him to his knees. At a regal five-ten, Samantha Dillon was already taller than her five-eight husband, Ted. But she loomed like a Goddess when she stood in her high-heeled bedroom slippers above her kneeling mate. She paused to look in the mirror, pleased with what she saw. Although in her early 40's she still had the looks and body of a thirty year old. A mane of dark brown hair fell to creamy white shoulders and her green eyes caught the light in a metallic shimmer that enhanced their color and depth. The mirror revealed the creature at her feet, naked save for his collar and a plastic chastity device. *Won't be needing 'that' any more.* Her left hand held the pink leather handle of a chain leash, its other end firmly affixed to the stiff, pink posture collar around the neck of her husband.

Husband? Well, on paper – legally. Now…now he's my slave, my obedient and willing slave. In her mind Ted Dillon was rapidly sinking away. He still had a bit of a paunch, but even that was disappearing, now that she had him on a strict diet and exercise regime. His hair was starting to grow and his eyebrows were carefully plucked. Some women in his office had remarked on his new *look*, but the men were oblivious, thinking he was simply turning into some sort of neat freak. *Tedi is what he will become, my androgynous sissy slut, devoting his life, his very existence – to ME.*

She gave the leash another tug and led her crawling husband to the boudoir chair in the corner of the bedroom, HER bedroom, having long ago removed him to a smaller bedroom. A cursory inspection revealed that he had prepared the scene according to her instructions: crystal dish, manicure scissors, cigarettes, ash tray, chilled water and cell phone.

She took her seat in the exquisite chair of carved mahogany and rich brocade fabric. Her hand tugged his leash, pulling him forward as she slowly spread her legs and led his face to within inches of her bushy mound. "Oh yes, I know how much you want this," she chided. "But this, *this* is a clean pussy, baby, fresh from the bath. Do sissy sluts get clean pussies?"

His eyes never met hers; instead they were transfixed to the shiny brown hairs before him. The scent of her sex mixed with that of her bath soap, and he felt his cock struggle fruitlessly in its plastic confines. He shook his head back and forth, acknowledging that he understood he'd forever lost access to his wife…and to his own sex.

"Sluts get left-overs." She reached down to pat his head; he was her pet, her toy. "And cuckolds get cream pies - don't they?"

He nodded again, the movement of his head wafting her scent around him. He felt as if he would go mad with desire – and frustration.

"Be a good slut, get me ready for my date, serve us well, and you'll get your cuckold baptism – just like I promised." Her hand dipped into the folds of her sex and she slowly stroked herself. She watched his eyes, all his emotions were in his eyes and she could read them like a book. "You must prepare the pussy – and prepare me."

He nodded slowly; his body shook uncontrollably. His desire made his cock swell, as much as it could, and the chastity device hideously stood out from his groin.

Samantha didn't need to look to know what was happening to him. She controlled his every action and emotion when she wanted. She pulled a moist finger from her fiery slit and rubbed the essence under his nose. It was hard for her not to laugh and spoil the moment when she saw him swoon at her gift. "A smell is all you get. Now take the scissors and trim my pubic hairs. Remember, you're making my pussy presentable, all nice and neat, for Collin. It's your gift, your wife's pussy, to your former employee." She laughed at the situation, her poor wimp of a husband humiliated by serving up his wife as a gift for a former subordinate. "Be very careful with those scissors, do a neat job, and put all the clippings in the dish."

She lit a cigarette and exhaled, watching the blue smoke envelop the head of her slave. Everything was going exactly as planned, her carefully choreographed path of humiliation and degradation for her most willing slave. She picked up the phone and punched in a number.

"Hello – I'm fine – I'm here with your big brother."

He grimaced; she was talking to Karen, his younger sister – step sister – who'd always been a pain for him.

"Of course he's gagged, who'd be interested in hearing anything he has to say – the inflatable one, he hates it – I don't know, I'll ask."

She grabbed his leash and jerked on it, pulling his head up. "Baby sister wants me to give the gag a couple of pumps, in her honor. You don't mind do you?" The despair in his eyes made her smile, *how hopeless his situation is; I love it!* "Here Karen, I'll hold the phone up to him."

Once more she held the malevolent pump before

his eyes, taunting him, teasing him, making him wait for that horrid rush of air that would further stretch his already swollen mouth. She squeezed the pump. Once. Twice.

His squeals and "mmpphh, mmpphh" elicited howls of laughter from the women.

"Serves the shit right," Karen said, "payback is hell, and it won't stop. So, you doing the whole thing tonight, like you told me?"

"Of course, I love it when a plan comes together. He's trimming my hair now. A picture? Sure" Samantha held out her phone, "Smile for sister."

Ted looked up and forced the best smile he could through the gag.

There was a flash and Samantha was back on the phone. "It's on its way to you, and he looks so precious. Sure I can send a copy to your mother as well." She watched his shoulders sag with the resignation that his humiliation would reach no limits. "Yes, Collin is coming for me at seven, and we have Teddi's evening all planned out. No, we don't need a babysitter tonight, but we are planning a weekend get-away in another month or so, do you want him then?"

Samantha couldn't see it, but at the mention of spending a weekend being tended to by his step-sister and step-mother Ted cringed, his ass clenched and his ball sack trembled in sheer terror.

"Oh yes," Samantha lit another cigarette and watched as her slave meticulously trimmed her pubic hairs, carefully placing the clippings in the crystal dish. "He'll be thoroughly cock trained in all his openings before I leave him with you. Whatever you want. Naked or clothed - sure, I'll send him with some of his uniforms.

Guests? As long as they're tested and safe I see no problem, otherwise have them use condoms."

She lifted her legs over the arms of the chair to allow her slave to trim the lower hairs. "A bridge party next week? No, sorry I can't make it. But give your mother my best. Teddi? A serving maid? I don't see why not. How many will be attending? Twelve? Well that's certainly going to keep him busy and on his toes. Oh yes, he's becoming quite adept in his heels. Five inch, but we're starting on six inches soon. Probably ballet heels, but for display only, after all, he does have to be productive, otherwise what use is he?"

Though he had no idea what would come next, it was usually never anything good, Ted was glad when Samantha ended the call.

She jerked on his leash and ordered him to fetch a mirror. He crawled away and returned, on his hands and knees, and held out the mirror to his Mistress.

Samantha looked over her newly trimmed pussy and pointed out places that needed additional work. *All in all, he did a rather good job, but I'm never going to tell the little shit anything like that.* "Kneel up!" she commanded.

He quickly assumed the 'kneel up' position: knees spread, revealing his chastised cock and exposed balls, ready to be kicked or stepped on, hands clasped behind his back, head up, ready to be slapped or stuffed with a cock, and his chest out, exposing the nipples that he loved to have stroked. Blissfully, no punishment was forthcoming; instead her hands went to the back of his head to unlock the wretched inflatable gag. He sighed when her beautiful fingers opened the valve to deflate the rubber intruder.

"Better?" she cooed.

He nodded and stretched his aching jaw. He watched as she opened her nightstand drawer and removed a package, obviously a gift, wrapped in pink paper and finished off with a lavender bow.

"Collin bought you a present." The voice was pleasant, but still held that ominous dread for him. A present? Whether it was from Samantha or Collin, it couldn't be good, nothing ever was.

He put out his hands and tentatively accepted the gift. "T-Thank you…Mistress."

Once more her hand, that soft silky hand that could also punish, stroked his cheek. "Open it, baby, let me see your present."

Tedi's hands shook as he removed the paper and opened the box revealing a large and lifelike penis. He slowly lifted it from the box, impressed by its size: the length, the girth and the heft he felt in his hand. The bulbous head was smooth, and the shaft covered with thick veins. He had no idea of the size, but it was obviously larger, much larger, than his own organ, not that he'd had that in his hands for quite some time.

He felt her close, her hot breath in his ear. "It's Collin's," she whispered.

His head whipped around to look at her, his eyebrows knotted in confusion.

"A copy," she mewed. She took it from his hands and lovingly stroked it, caressed her cheek with it. "Such a lovely cock. That's what men have – cocks. What do you have?"

His head dropped. "A clitty," he mumbled.

"What? Say it again," she ordered.

He looked up at her, "Sissy sluts have clitties."

She held out the lifelike cock, using the bulbous head to trace lines on his face. "That's right, yours isn't big enough to be a cock, you have a clitty." She laughed and rapped him on the nose with the cock. "That's why I need," she hit him again, "this. This – makes me happy. And it will make you happy too – after you learn to pleasure it. It's made from a mold of Collin's cock. Isn't it dreamy?"

"Yes, Mistress."

"Kiss it." She held it to his lips. "Look at me while you do it."

He leaned forward to place his lips on the giant cock before him, his eyes locked to those of his Mistress.

"Keep looking at me, always look at the owner of the cock you are servicing; show the owner how you adore the cock you are worshipping. Give it light butterfly kisses."

Tedi kissed the cock, watched Samantha and tried to ignore the throbbing of his own cock. *Am I gay? Is she turning me into a homosexual? What does she want from me?*

She slowly rubbed the cock over his lips. "Flick the tip of your tongue over the head, Collin likes that."

The idea of being on his knees, with Collin's cock in his face made him shake. With fear? With excitement?

"Now open, prepare to fully enjoy the Alpha Male cock."

He didn't know if he could take the monster into his mouth and considered the dreaded inflatable gag to be preferable to this giant invader.

Her fingers found his nipple again, stroking, coaxing him. "Come on, baby, do it for me. Pleasuring my lover's cock will please me. You want to please me don't you? Make me happy?"

He nodded and opened his mouth to the cock.

She smiled.; with his clitty locked away his nipples became an extreme source of pleasure: her strength, his weakness. She'd soon make them, and his ass, the center of his erotic world. "Open." She slid the cock head past his lips. "Run your tongue over it, get familiar with it, you'll learn to love how it feels, how it tastes. Look at me."

His eyes looked up, but seemed to look past her, as if in a daze.

"Relax, I'm going to push it in a bit further, relax and breathe." She felt him flinch as she pushed the phallic wonder further into his mouth. "Hold still, breathe."

His eyes filled with panic; he feared he'd choke to death on the cock and breathed with relief as she slowly removed it.

She wiped the cock over his face, smearing him with his own saliva. *He needs to get used to that.* "We're going to do it again, eventually you'll have to be able to take it all, Collin likes it like that, when he can put it all the way in a slut's mouth. You'll gag sometimes; that's OK. A lot of men like to make sluts gag on their cock." *And I'm definitely going to enjoy watching you gag on a cock.* "OK, open; we're going in further this time."

After a few more practice sessions, Samantha left the cock in her slut's mouth and relaxed in her chair. "Keep sucking on that the rest of the afternoon. Believe me, the faster you get used to handling that, the better off you'll be, just a warning." She lit another cigarette. "Tonight is your official entrance into being a Cuckold."

She lifted a long and sensuous leg to his chest and used her toes to tweak his nipples. "You don't need to know everything that's going to happen, but there are a few things that I'll tell you, things that I expect you to do in EXACTLY the way I tell you to do them. First, when Collin arrives…"

Sissy Tedi stood facing the corner. The *cuckold evening* called for full sissy maid regalia and Samantha had spared no expense in preparing her sissy maid husband for the ultimate initiation. Layers of crisp, white petticoats held the short black and white maid's dress almost horizontal. The short length did nothing to preserve modesty and the garter tabs extending from the severe corset were clearly visible. When Tedi bent to serve, as was required, his caged clitty was on display. Black, seamed fishnet stockings and black, patent stiletto heels enclosed the sissy's legs and feet. The top of the maid's dress was low enough to expose a hint of nipple and the cruelly laced corset pushed Tedi's breasts into an almost feminine shape. A black, page boy wig framed a face that was excessively made up. White lace gloves, choker and headpiece completed the outfit.

Tedi balanced on the stilettos, conscious to stifle any excessive movement. When Mistress Samantha said to 'remain still' she meant it, and would punish offenses against her edict with strokes of the cane. Even though his legs were cramping and feet hurt, Tedi was relieved that his mouth was free of any intruder – at least for now. The snap of a finger focused his attention.

"You will dress me."

Tedi turned and curtsied, a skill learned under the tutelage of Mistress Theodora. Samantha sent Tedi to her for two weeks of intensive, brutal training. On his return Tedi was much more submissive and docile, with a surprising array of new and useful skills.

Samantha smiled at her project: *If only women knew about the advantages of a sissy maid, then every woman would have at least one and the world would have either Alpha Males – or sissy maids.* "Garter belt."

Her sissy maid picked up the black, wispy garment and delicately fastened it about Samantha's waist. Stockings were next, and she sat and extended a leg as Tedi slowly rolled the sheer and expensive stockings up Samantha's legs. She couldn't help but chuckle as she watched Tedi's shaking hands. "Turns you on, does it? Well, you always did want me to wear garter belts and stockings and high heels. And now I do – for other men. Collin loves it; he thinks it's incredibly sexy. And you *do* get to see me dressed like this, so you get your little thrill as well – don't you?"

"Yes, Mistress."

Poor thing, so crushed, helping me dress sexy for my date, sending me me off to have sex with others. Bad for him, good for me. "Panties. Collin likes me to wear my panties over the stockings and garter belt so I can take off the panties but keep on the rest when we make love. Don't you think that's sexy?"

"Yes, Mistress."

"Bra."

Tedi slipped the bra on her and fastened the back. It was an exquisite bra, matching the expensive panties.

"Hand me the dress, and then bring me the black pumps, the stilettos."

When Tedi returned with the shoes Samantha was putting the finishing touches on her dress. She sat and extended a leg as Tedi knelt to slip the designer shoes on her feet. She extended a foot and her sissy maid obediently kissed the sole. *It's wonderful when they're so well trained.* She turned to her dressing table and began applying her makeup. "There's iced tea in the carafe. Pour yourself a glass and drink it down."

It was an unusual order, but Tedi was too well trained to question or disobey. He poured a glass, there was only one large glass available, and drank it down.

Samantha applied her mascara and eyeliner. "Another."

Tedi poured and drank another glass.

She carefully selected earrings and a necklace, and pulled leather gloves from a drawer on her dressing table, "Still thirsty?"

A reply to a question was always expected – a quick and polite reply; there was never time to plan a response or plot all the various consequences. Not that it mattered, a response could be twisted any number of ways. "No, Mistress – thank you Mistress."

She pulled on the leather gloves; she knew how it excited him. Slowly she smoothed them over her forearms; they came almost to her elbow. "Another."

"Yes, Mistress." He poured and drank his third large glass of iced tea; he felt bloated, but knew that bathroom privileges required permission. SHE would decide if, and when, he needed such relief.

She busied herself putting items into a small beaded clutch. "Wait downstairs for Collin – and remember what we discussed."

"Yes, Mistress." He executed a deep curtsey, but she paid it no mind. She didn't have to look to know he would curtsey and obey; he'd been trained to do that.

Once more he found himself standing – waiting – to serve – and obey. The five inch heels were making his calves ache and the pointed-toe pumps cramped his feet. She inflicted her pain and control with his wardrobe. Still, to complain was to invite something worse. *Maybe she'll simply go on her date, have sex with Collin and leave me alone for the evening.* He knew better; hope was something she was slowly stripping away, ripping it from his psyche and trampling it to death under her spike heels. And she enjoyed making him watch; even participate, in the spectacle.

The doorbell brought him back to reality and he took a quick moment to straighten out his billowing skirt and fluff his petticoats. As he opened the door he curtseyed his greeting, "Welcome to Mistress Samantha's house." He backed away as Collin Blake sauntered into the room. Even in his five inch heels, Tedi was dwarfed by the imposing six-four Collin. "May I take your coat sir?" It never occurred to Tedi how ridiculous the situation was: his servitude as a feminized sissy maid to one who'd recently been his professional subordinate. Such things rarely entered Tedi's mind any more, his objective, his raison d'être was survival, getting through the day while avoiding as much punishment and humiliation as possible. He gingerly accepted Master Collin's coat and stood still as the Alpha Male circled, taking in the total sissy splendor before him.

"Samantha has done quite a job with you. She told me all about it, but…" He removed a small digital camera from his pocket. "Hang up my coat and we'll go to the living room; I want some pictures, for the office."

Dread coursed through Tedi again; it was an all-too-familiar feeling. But instinctive training took over, and he quickly hung up the coat and followed Master Collin to the living room.

Collin pointed to a place in the middle of the room. "Face away from me and bend over. Turn – a bit – now look back at me. I want your ass, your chastised clitty, and your face all in the picture. Smile, say 'I want a big 'ol cock in my mouth.'"

Tedi did his best to comply; a bad behavior report to Mistress Samantha would mean punishment. FLASH!

"Say it again; I want a video clip as well as a still picture, and say it nice and loud."

"I want a big 'ol cock in my mouth!"

Collin adjusted the camera for playback and nodded approvingly. "One more, and wiggle your ass while you beg for that cock."

Tedi put on his best smile and seductively wiggled his ass. "I want a big 'ol cock in my mouth!" FLASH!

Collin took Tedi through several poses, both innocent and decadent, and finally satisfied, he put the camera away, "Scotch, neat."

Tedi minced away in his heels to fetch the drink while Collin relaxed on the sofa.

Tedi returned with the drink resting on a silver serving tray. He served in the manner he'd been instructed: stiff-legged, bending at the waist to display his décolleté and expose his bottom. Collin took the drink and allowed Tedi to hold the humiliating posture for several seconds before dismissing the sissy slave with a wave of his hand. Tedi scurried off to put the tray away, return and curtsey, his domestic task complete.

Collin snapped his fingers and pointed to the floor and Tedi quickly knelt, obediently following the non-verbal command.

"Thank you for the gift, Sir," Tedi said. His eyes moved to the box on the coffee table.

"You like it then?" Collin sipped his drink and eyed the kneeling sissy maid.

"Oh yes, Sir. It's so big!" Tedi played out the scene exactly as Mistress had directed. "I love the way it fills my mouth."

"Really? I'd like to see that. I'd be impressed if you can take it all."

Tedi tried his best to show his excitement, although humiliation and shame were the emotions he really felt. He opened the box and took out the massive pole. Holding it before his face he ran his lace-gloved hands over the shaft, brought it to his lips, stuck out his tongue and lapped at the head. "Mmmmmm."

Collin couldn't help but feel his own cock quiver in excitement. As an Alpha Male Bull he had no qualms about another male sucking his cock, there'd been several submissive male sissy maid husbands who'd been broken on his massive tool. This one looked more ready than most, *Hell, he might even be eager for it.*

Tedi's lips parted and the cock made its entrance. With his tongue slathering over the shaft to lubricate it, he moved the phallic invader slowly in and out, deeper each time. His eyes never left those of Collin, following Mistress's dictum to 'look at the male, show your love for his cock with your eyes.'

Collin smiled, he was pleased with this one; it was going to be fun turning this one into a true cuck. He reached forward, grabbed the back of Tedi's head and put his other hand on the base of the cock. "Show me slut; show me what you can do."

Tedi batted his eyelashes, hideous long false ones, and took a deep breath. He felt the cock enter – deeper – deeper – until it hit the back of his throat. He literally choked down the panic and tried to remain still and calm. It was NOT a good time to upset Master.

Collin's hands were firm, holding the cock in place. "Hold it, hold it." He felt Tedi tremble. He pushed it deeper still, wanting to see the slut gag on the cock.

Tedi shook and gagged, tried to pull away, but the Alpha Male was too strong. He gagged again and Collin pulled the cock from his mouth.

Collin wiped the drool from the cock on Tedi's face, the next time that drool would contain a load of spunk. "Not bad, an acceptable start; but you're going to learn to take it all, for as long as I want it in there."

"I see you two are getting along well." Samantha stood at the top of the stairs, a vision of beauty and elegance. The black dress and mink wrap spoke of rich elegance, while the black stilettos and long leather gloves added a fetish edge to her look.

Collin stuck the cock in Tedi's mouth and rose to

greet Samantha, extending his arm to help her down the stairs.

They do make a striking couple Tedi thought. At five-ten, and with her five inch heels, Samantha was almost as tall as Collin. They'd surely be the most eye catching couple wherever they went tonight.

Samantha walked to the kneeling Tedi and patted him on the head. "She likes your present; she's had it in and out of her mouth all day; haven't you?"

Tedi nodded and pulled the cock from his mouth. "Oh yes, Mistress, I love sucking this cock."

"I took some pictures earlier, maybe I could get some more?" Collin took the camera from his pocket again.

"Of course, a splendid idea, pictures to mark the occasion, my sissy's first cuckold date."

For the next several minutes, the trio posed for a variety of pictures: Tedi kissing Samantha's feet, Tedi kneeling and sucking the cock she held, sucking the cock as held by Collin, pictures of Samantha and Collin in each other's arms.

Samantha looked at the pictures as Collin displayed them on the camera. "Lovely." She turned to Tedi, "Tomorrow you will print these out. Make four photo albums, one for me, Collin, your sister and your mother. I'm sure everyone will enjoy them. And make a DVD of all the video clips, copies for everyone."

Tedi meekly nodded. His humiliation obviously knew no boundaries.

"Excuse me," Collin turned to go to the bathroom.

"You're doing very well this evening," Samantha said.

Tedi smiled at the praise – until he felt the full

weight of the leather-gloved hand slapping his face.

"Don't get cocky!" The hand found his face again, another vicious slap which jerked his head from one side to the other and sent one of his clip-on earrings flying across the room. "You DON'T want to make this any worse than it's going to be."

"N – n- no, I mean y – yes, Mistress."

Collin emerged from the bathroom and walked to them. He gave Samantha a little kiss on the cheek, "Your turn."

She smiled that smile that always chilled Tedi to his marrow, and went to the bathroom.

"Up slut!" Collin snapped his fingers. "Over there," he pointed to a closet door.

Tedi walked to the door while Collin removed a box from an end table drawer. Obviously, the evening had been carefully planned by Samantha and Collin. They'd left nothing to chance in their meticulously staged cuckold initiation.

Collin handed Tedi a lubricated condom and a vibrating egg, whose long cord ended in a black box. "Do I need to tell you where this goes?"

Tedi curtsied, "No, Master." He ripped opened the condom, inserted the egg and bent over to shove it up his ass.

"Wait," chuckled Collin, waving a finger and holding his camera. "Pictures, remember? Look at me and smile as you shove it in, be happy."

He did his best to smile at the camera as his fingers parted his ass cheeks and he felt the egg slip inside. FLASH! FLASH!

Collin kicked a box across the floor, the box coming to rest at Tedi's feet. "Another present, aren't you the lucky slut?"

Tedi's "Yes, Master," was preceded by the obligatory curtsey. He opened the box. *Shoes, these must be six inches.*

It was as if Collin read his mind. "Six and a half inches, with no platform, quite a hideous arch…yes? But Samantha and I decided it was time to take you to the next level. Put them on."

It was a struggle; the shoes were new, with incredibly high heels and an extreme pointed toe. Tedi finally got them on and precariously stood in place, adjusting to the increased height and the way it altered his center of balance. "T – thank you, Master."

Collin ignored the thanks, his attention focused on securing two over-the-door restraints to the top of the door then closing it. He tugged on the restraints and nodded approvingly at their security. "Back up, cucky, hands over your head."

With small, uncertain steps Tedi backed up to the door and extended his hands to the top as Collin efficiently secured them. "Comfy?" Collin teased.

"No, Master."

"Not my concern. Did you actually think we'd let you have an evening to yourself?"

Well, yes, that's what I'd hoped. "I serve at Mistress's and Master's will."

"Good answer." Collin pulled down the top of Tedi's maid's dress, exposing his tiny bust and nipples. He took the tender buds in his hands and squeezed them, noting with satisfaction how Tedi went weak at the knees, "Never seen a sissy slut who didn't swoon at that, especially after a few weeks in chastity." He gently stroked the nipples, "You'd let me do that all night – wouldn't you?"

"Oh yes, Master, please."

Collin cruelly pinched them and Tedi went rigid with the pain. "Samantha and I decide if and when you get pleasure." He pinched harder, making Tedi squeal. "You control nothing, we control everything."

"Yes, Master, I'm sorry."

"Recognize these?" Collin held forth a set of Japanese Clover Clamps, diabolical nipple clamps that pinched tighter whenever pressure was applied to their chain.

"Yes, Master." Tedi winced as first one, then the other was cruelly applied to his nipples.

Collin toyed with the chain, delighting in the reactions he coaxed from Tedi's pained face when the clicking of her stilettos announced Samantha's arrival.

"Having fun?" she laughed.

Collin cruelly jerked the chain, making Tedi yelp. "One of us is."

Samantha walked forward, "Let's finish up here."

Collin moved to the big screen TV across the room, as Samantha took her place in front of the hapless sissy maid. She brought a large sports bottle to his cheek; it was warm. When she pulled the bottle away he saw it was filled with a yellow fluid. She wafted the bottle under his nose and the acrid smell of piss made him recoil. She laughed, "Another gift from Collin and me – we do spoil you."

Tedi watched in expectant terror as each of his two antagonists busied themselves with various tasks. Collin was hooking wires and items to the TV. Samantha attached a large rubber-like tubing to his chastity device and plugged the other end of the hose into a hole in the top of the sports bottle. A second hose connected to the sports bottle was shoved in his mouth, with Samantha taping the tube to his cheek to keep it in place. Her last act was to slide the piss bottle into a holder with a length of chain attached. She turned to Collin, "How much do you think this bottle weighs?"

Collin shrugged his shoulders, "Couple a pounds."

She turned to smile at Tedi. Slowly, she picked up the chain to the nipple clamps and fastened it to the chain holding the bottle.

Ted's eyes went wide, his head frantically shaking 'no'.

She tested the weight of the bottle in her hand, then slowly let the length of the chain play out until the bottle fell to his knees. Another inch was in her fingers, then the full weight would be applied to the evil clamps.

She let the bottle go, for an instant, to show him the pain, and then pulled it back. "Yes, it's going to hurt. My advice is that you reduce the weight of the bottle. Drink fast and deep my slut. Keeping that bottle empty is a way to minimize at least some of the pain."

That's why she made me drink the three glasses of tea and deny me bathroom privileges. Tedi's bladder was already bursting, and now they were leaving him with a dilemma: drink the piss to relieve the nipple torment, but his bladder was already full, so he'd end up emptying himself back into the bottle. It was hopeless.

Samantha let the full weight of the bottle rest on the chain and Tedi screamed. "I told you – drink – suck it all up." She smiled, a smug smile of victory as his cheeks started moving in and out and the yellow liquid moved up the tube into his mouth. "He's doing it!"

Collin moved in front of Tedi and took yet another picture. "Did you ever doubt that he would?"

"No, but still, it's so exciting to do it to him."

Collin punched buttons on his cell phone and suddenly a picture of the piss drinking Tedi flashed on the big screen TV. Collin pointed at the TV. "There you are cucky, in all your piss drinking glory. We'll be sending you pictures of our evening out, us having a good time while you break in those new heels and recycle piss. Nothing to say?"

Samantha laughed, "I think he's too busy trying to empty that bottle to take the time to thank us."

When Collin punched in a second text message the vibrating egg came to life. He and Samantha watched as Tedi writhed from the anal excitement. His movements caused the piss bottle to sway, further straining his mauled nipples. He teetered on the skyscraper heels. His entire environment was designed to torment.

"Best to stay absolutely still, and keep drinking up the contents of that bottle," Samantha advised. "Keep watching the TV. Oh, and enjoy your evening."

Tedi watched as Collin helped Samantha with her mink wrap, took her arm and escorted her out the door. His wife / Mistress was off on her official cuckold date – and he was left to suffer – and wait. He sucked more piss, he needed to empty the bottle – relieve the pain on his nipples, but he couldn't hold back the urge and released his bladder. As the bottle slowly pulled on his nipples he began to suck. By the end of the evening any reservations against drinking piss would be overcome. *Maybe that's what she wants, or maybe she simply wants to torment me.*

The first call came twenty minutes after the lovers departed. The phone rang five times and Tedi heard the answering machine pick up. "Is your bottle empty? Have the urge to pee? Decisions, decisions!" The phone's electronics didn't disguise either the glee or derision in Samantha's voice. "We're almost at the restaurant, anticipating a lovely dinner and fine wine. Are you enjoying *your* vintage? We'll send you some pictures, for your new cucky scrapbook." The line went dead and moments later the vibrating egg came to life. Tedi was startled by the sensation and nearly lost his balance on the treacherous heels.

From his high-heeled perch Tedi watched the mantle clock and its progress seemed agonizingly slow. It was going to be a long night. He tried to flex his toes and move his feet; the killer shoes were beginning to exact their terror. Every breath he exhaled brought the smell of piss to his nostrils; his lips and tongue tasted of it. He thought about brushing his teeth and using mouthwash, *if she'll allow it.*

The bloom of light from the flat screen TV caught his attention and a phone picture of Samantha and Collin filled the screen. They were seated at a cozy corner booth, the high leather seating giving them privacy for... They held up wine glasses and smiled at the camera, *me, they're smiling at, laughing at, me.* The glossy white china plates and gleaming silver flatware were in stark contrast to the bottle of piss suspended from his nipples. It was a rueful reminder of his new status, his existence until Mistress Samantha decided otherwise.

The vibrating egg and the telephone seemed to go off in unison. When the machine picked up it was Samantha. "Hey, sweetie, having a good time? This new restaurant is marvelous. We're going to enjoy a lovely supper and then go dancing, stop in a few clubs. When we get home we'll make you an official cuck, OK? Think about that magnificent cock of Collin's and how you're going to beg him to pleasure me with it. Think of something good to say while you're *hanging out* at home. We want you to be sincere in your need to be a cucky." The phone line went dead, but the egg vibrated for another five minutes.

They'd planned and executed an interminable existence for him, while the lovers dined and flirted he suffered their carefully choreographed round of indignities. If that wasn't enough, the next call chilled him to the bone – his step sister.

"Hey big brother, Samantha sent me some pictures, very nice, hope you're planning to wear that cute little outfit when you serve at Mom's bridge party. That should be a hoot! Are you there, or are you tied up? He-he-he. Don't Samantha and Collin make the hottest couple? Geez, she never looked that good with you. I hope you enjoy your evening. I expect to hear all about it, every detail, next time we're together. Did I tell you? Gillian and I are planning our own little evening with you. Bye-bye."

Gillian, my step-sister's Lesbian lover; that's one cruel and vindictive bitch. He didn't have time to dwell on thoughts of suffering under their hands. His eyes were drawn to the next image to appear on the TV.

It was Samantha and Collin, still in the restaurant, this time in a deep embrace, his hand in her dress groping her breasts. *The waiter must have taken the picture*. Their shameless display indicated they had no qualms about his public humiliation.

A second picture quickly followed. It showed Samantha holding the digital camera and showing the cocktail waitress a picture of Tedi sucking the copy of Collin's cock. He shifted his weight, gingerly, to ease the pain in his feet without setting the sports bottle to moving. He knew that when they removed the nipple clamps and the blood flowed back in…it was going to hurt. *No doubt they'll get off on that too.*

The picture faded from the screen, *How is Collin doing that?* and he prepared himself for the next onslaught of the vibrating egg. It didn't come; there was only the sound of the ticking mantle clock. He waited – nothing. *Maybe the batteries died?*

He relaxed and tried to focus, tried NOT to think about peeing, although his bladder was once again begging for relief. The egg went off, once again making him jump. The phone rang; it was Collin, "WE are in control slut, always – never forget that. Your only options are to obey and endure, anything else just makes it worse for you."

The hours dragged on, filled with teasing phone calls, his ass violated by the egg, and an endless array of pictures of Collin and Samantha enjoying a romantic evening. Past midnight car headlights cast shadows through the room and he heard the crunch of the tires on the driveway and the whir of the garage door opener. *Please let it end soon.*

Their laughter preceded them, their gaiety a sharp contrast to his misery. Samantha still looked beautiful. Despite the torments, humiliation and abuse he was captivated by her beauty, held spell-bound. Her brown hair was still perfectly coiffed, her green eyes sparkling – with lust? Evil? She'd shed her mink wrap in the hallway, but the black cocktail dress and the leather gloves gave her the look of a chic and elegant tormentress. Her right hand held a long cigarette holder in an underhanded grip. She looked like something out of Vogue – the Dungeon issue.

She silently smoked, blowing the plumes of smoke into his face. Even then, he never averted his eyes, longingly gazing at her through a blue-gray cloud. Her gloved hand swatted his piss bottle, setting it dangling from the tortured nipples. "Empty. I bet it wasn't empty all night, was it?"

He shook his head 'no'.

"We're going to release you," she saw hope glimmer in his eyes. *I'll fucking kill THAT!* "The highlight of the evening is yet to come; you still have to offer me to Collin. And make it sincere."

He eagerly nodded 'yes'.

"Collin will release you from the door and remove the nipple clamps, scream if you like. The shoes stay on. Go to the bathroom and use the toilet and brush your teeth; we don't want Collin putting that marvelous cock of his in a dirty little mouth – do we?"

"No, Mistress. I'll do as you say," he mumbled through the tube in his mouth.

She cocked her head and furrowed her eyebrows.

"Of course you'll do as I say. What a stupid thing to say." She yanked on the nipple chain, eliciting the most pitiful wail. "Do you think before you speak?"

"Ohhhh, I'm sorrrrry, Mistress."

The clicking of her heels down the hallway was her only response and soon the large figure of Master Collin filled his view. "You shouldn't piss her off." His hand reached for one of the clover clamps, "Better take a deep breath, I'll remove it on three. One – two." He removed the clamp, one beat before Tedi was prepared.

"Awww – ohhh." The pain was more than he'd anticipated. Suddenly the other clamp was removed and the pain rippled through his chest, his nipples burning as if they'd been set afire.

Collin laughed, "You're still so gullible, months after being enslaved and domesticated. Don't you get it? We do what we want." He unfastened Tedi's wrists, ripped the tape from Tedi's cheek and removed the tube from his mouth.

Tedi shakily stood on the skyscraper heels, his nipples burning, rubbing his arms in an attempt to breathe new life into them.

Collin handed him the nipple clamps and the piss bottle. "Go clean up and then come to us, we'll be waiting in the living room."

"Yes, Master." Tedi turned to walk away and nearly fell down. He'd never yet walked in his new shoes. Cautiously, he made his way down the hall and into the bathroom.

Master Collin's voice boomed after him, "Not too long cucky, we have need of you."

Tedi fell to the toilet seat; it was good to be off his feet, if only for a few minutes. Before he sat down he'd filled his mouth with mouthwash, spit and filled it again. He worked the minty liquid throughout his mouth while he pissed an unending golden flow. A cold washcloth provided some small comfort to his abused nipples. He feared he'd been permanently damaged. He stood, spit out the mouthwash and brushed his teeth. On shaky legs, *these heels are impossibly high*, he made his way down the hall – to offer his wife to Collin – to serve the lovers – to complete the cuckold date for Mistress.

Not surprisingly, he found them cuddling on the couch, Collin's hand up her dress, caressing her thigh. Tedi's mind raced, he needed to stay on script, Samantha wanted this to go HER way.

He minced before the lovers and curtsied, nearly falling to his face from the spindly heels.

Collin laughed, "He's going to need some practice in those shoes."

Samantha snuggled closer to her lover, "I'll keep him in them the rest of the weekend. It'll be good training – won't it cucky?"

His second curtsey was better. "Yes, Mistress." He dropped to his knees before Collin. "Thank you for dating Mistress Samantha tonight. I hope you both enjoyed your-selves."

Collin's hand moved over Samantha's breast and she purred her delight. "It was an enjoyable evening. Samantha is a delightful and beautiful woman."

"Yes, Master. Will you please pleasure her with your cock? It's much bigger than mine; I'm sure you both would enjoy it."

Collin appeared to give it thought. "Perhaps…but

I'd like to see what I'm getting - full disclosure."

Samantha brought her full lips down on his, smothering him in a passionate kiss. Slowly she broke the kiss and slid from the sofa, a seductive temptress, a serpent of desire. "Anything you want, lover."

She stood before him, in her five-inch heels she towered over the nervous Tedi who knelt before the expectant lovers. "Present your Mistress," she commanded.

Tedi rose to his feet and gave a curtsey. He moved behind Samantha and unzipped her dress.

Samantha shook her shoulders and the dress slid to the floor, pooling like molten crepe at her high-heeled feet. Her hands placed sensuously on her hips, she slowly pirouetted, clad only in her garter belt, stockings, panties, bra and the wicked long leather gloves and spike heels. "Like what you see, lover?"

"Most assuredly," Collin smiled. "Keep on the stockings, garter belt, heels and gloves."

"Mmm, male authority, so sexy. See, cucky, that's a man who knows what he wants, if you'd been that much of a man you wouldn't be where you are now." She snapped her fingers and Tedi gently unhooked her bra. Samantha removed it, striptease fashion, held it out at arm's length, and let it fall into Collin's lap.

He picked up the wispy, black lace and brought it to his nose, taking in her captivating scent.

Tedi moved behind his Mistress and cupped his hands around her breasts, extending them forward, offering them… "Please, Sir, have you ever seen breasts more beautiful, more ready to love and be loved? Won't you please pleasure them, Sir?"

Samantha felt herself shiver with excitement. This was even more erotic than she'd imagined; her husband, her slave, offering her up to another man, begging the man to pleasure her. She felt her slave kneel, his shaking fingers pulling her panties down her stockinged legs.

"Please, Master, this pussy longs for a real cock, something I cannot provide. Master's cock is what she needs."

Samantha licked her lips, and let her gloved hands trace a line from her neck, between her breasts and down to her moist channel. "Our little cucky trimmed up my bush, so tidy, you like?"

Collin eagerly nodded. He was enjoying the spectacle, Samantha's little show and tell, but he was anxious to consummate the cuckold ceremony.

Samantha grabbed Tedi by the hair and pulled his face close to her mound. "Cucky wanted to eat me, didn't you? But I told him that cucks don't get clean, fresh pussies, only used ones, second helpings, cream pies. But I have a treat for you." Her free hand reached down to a crystal dish that Tedi, in his excitement, hadn't noticed. "Open wide," she pulled his head back by his hair and dropped a handful of hairs into his waiting mouth. "These are from this morning, see, you do get to eat me." She gave a wicked laugh and Collin couldn't help but join in. Her gloved fingers gathered up another pinch of pubic hairs. "Ask for more, beg."

"Please, Mistress, may I please have more?"

She laughed as she dropped the last of the hairs in his mouth and watched as his tongue and lips worked to successfully swallow them.

Collin shook his head in amazement, "Samantha, you are too, too wicked."

"Now that you've had your treat, I want you to crawl to Master Collin and beg his cock to come out and play." She released her grip on his head and nudged him forward with the pointed toe of her high heel.

Tedi crawled forward and Collin conveniently spread his legs to allow Tedi to come fully nose-to-crotch.

"Please, Sir, may your wonderful cock pleasure Mistress?"

Collin winked at Samantha, who blew him a kiss. "Well, cucky, why don't you take it out and ask it yourself."

Tedi nervously unbuckled Collin's belt and unzipped his trousers. The massive cock, having been well teased, sprang from its enclosure, the size and suddenness of movement causing Tedi to shrink back. He felt Samantha's hand push his head back into position.

"Get closer cucky; it won't hurt you," she teased.

He took the throbbing shaft in his hands. It seemed bigger than its copy, and the real one had life to it: warmth, movement, it pulsed with heat and desire. He kissed the head, "Please, Master, please use this wonderful cock to pleasure Mistress and yourself."

His tongue flicked over the head, *Master Collin likes that*. He licked the first few inches and then slowly pulled it between his lips, feeling it fill his mouth.

Samantha's hand on the back of his head pushed him down further on the shaft. He felt her hot breath in his ear, smelled her musky scent, melted to her gloved hand softly stroking his tender nipple. "That's right, cucky, suck Master's cock, that's part of being a cuck, learning to take pleasure from Master's cock. It will pleasure both of us. You'll do this for all my lovers. It feels good, doesn't it, to have a cock in your mouth? To know you are preparing it for MY pleasure?"

Tedi was lost to the sensations: Samantha's scent and sultry voice, Master's large throbbing cock. He felt her pull him from the cock. "We don't want to waste this; after all, it's all about Collin and me. Your job is to get it ready, wet and hard – for me."

The two lovers stood and walked arm-in-arm upstairs as Tedi minced behind.

Tedi assisted Collin as he undressed, carefully hanging up Master's clothes. Samantha relaxed in her boudoir chair and enjoyed the spectacle of her submissive husband preparing her lover. *Life is good, it's good to be me.*

"That cock needs some attention. FLUFF," she commanded.

Tedi immediately took the cock into his mouth, licking and sucking, coaxing it back to size.

Samantha snapped her fingers. "Up, cucky!"

Tedi disengaged from the cock, a stream of drool hanging from his lips, and stood.

"One last item." Samantha held a black remote control unit in her hands. "Collin is quite creative and has used his engineering talents to create some – interesting – improvements to my bedchamber."

She pressed a button and a pallet smaller than a queen-sized bed rolled out from under Joanna's bed. There was a spread eagled human silhouette painted on the pallet and locking mechanisms at the wrist and ankle points. Samantha pressed another button and the restraints engaged and then disengaged. "We can lock you up and release you, by remote control. Clever, yes?"

"Yes, Mistress."

Collin inserted his life-like cock copy onto a rod affixed to the crotch region of the silhouette. With the press of another button the cock came to life.

"Get on, assume your position," Samantha ordered.

Tedi dropped to the floor and rolled over onto the pallet, placing his wrists and ankles in the designated spots. With the press of a button the restraints engaged. He felt something cold on his bottom. Collin was applying lube to his ass.

"Yes, we'll get you nice and lubed for tonight – as it's your first time." Samantha stood over him. "See we both get to enjoy Collin's marvelous cock. When we slide you under the bed you'll notice a small video display. You'll be able to see us making love, hear us, and feel the bed move, completely share in this wonderful experience."

Collin's arm snaked around Samantha, pulling her close and cupping her breast. "You spoil him."

Samantha smiled as her finger pressed a button, and Tedi's eyes went wide as the phallic intruder began its invasion. "I suppose I do, but he's such fun to have around." Once more she engaged the remote and the pallet began its slow withdrawal under the bed. She blew him a kiss as he faded from sight, "Nighty night, cucky."

END

Audra spun on one of her wicked heels and slowly walked the length of one of the wooden beams. Her hand lovingly caressed each intricately carved wooden phallus. "Today's game is Self-Impalement. Of course it would be easy for us to simply tie the creatures down," she glared over her shoulder at the slaves, "and fuck their sissy asses raw!" She quickly took on a softer tone, her words sweet and tender, "But how much more exquisite it is to make them commit the act themselves, to force their puckered openings over these shafts." The crowd nodded their approval as they watched Audra caress the largest of the wooden phalluses, her hand unable to fully grasp it.

Matriarch's Birthday

*S*he'd made a science of kicking males. Refined it. Developed it into an art. A religion of which she was the High Priestess and those males became the supplicants and objects of her unholy rites.

Her feet were the bane of male existence, cruel and unyielding – unforgiving. Her shoes – leather harbingers of pain and suffering. She'd spent a summer in Florence, enjoying the art, food, culture, and Italian men. Between cafés and museums she visited Carlo, shoemaker to the Dominant's Guild, that group of select women who ruled a world-wide underground matriarchy. He crafted the tools she used to terrorize and subjugate males.

Today Audra de Kranow wore the pumps, classic in detailing and styling, black kid leather. The five-inch heels were half gleaming chrome and rapier thin. Dangerous as those wicked heels were, it was the toes that held the terror. Carlo crafted a long and very pointed toe:

Italian leather taut and wrapped around a wooden form that kept the leather from buckling as it abused male flesh. Despite the long and pointed spear-like front, the toe box was set slightly further back and allowed the wearer a comfortable fit.

Audra stalked the corridor, her metal stilettos echoing on the concrete walls, heralding her approach to the males cowering in their cramped cells. She stopped at the door to the cell containing male number 19. When she entered the cell the slave quickly assumed his position at her feet. At five-ten in her five inch heels she loomed over the kneeling figure. She slowly backed away and circled the male, who remained in position. The only sounds were the clicking of her heels on the coarse concrete floor, the slapping of the crop on her palm, and the rapid breathing of the male at her feet.

She stopped behind him and stepped back. "Know what today is?"

It was a rhetorical question; she knew he didn't have the answer and she didn't care. Her right knee flexed and the wicked pointed toe of her stiletto found its mark in the soft flesh of his upper leg. Audra knew exactly where to kick, how much force to use, how to exact every ounce of pain without diminishing their capacity to do useful work – or accept more abuse.

Number 19 flinched at the pain, his yelp from the kneeling dog-like posture making him seem much like the lowly animal he'd become. But he'd been asked a direct question and was trained to respond, "N-n-no-, Mistress."

Poised like a ballerina on her left stiletto, perched on the rapier thin heel, her right leg whipped out twice more, each savage kick punctuated with her condemnation, "Stupid – stupid step daddy. It's Grand-Mum's birth-day."

She stepped back to observe the reddening skin, and made it a point to remember to look in on him again later, to see if the color of the bruises pleased her. She was meticulous in her work, following up, evaluating, refining her technique, the skin and musculature of her male victims the palette for the color of her abuses. She'd craft a patchwork of pain on this one before the day was through.

The hapless male shivered and whimpered, from the cold of his stark cell, from the pain, from the fear of the impending day. His daily existence had dulled his memories, all his cognitive abilities turned toward ensuring daily survival. Memories of halcyon days were distant, but the Matriarchal Birthday was an annual and singular horror not easily forgotten.

He heard her move and saw her gleaming stilettos appear poised over his splayed fingers, and he grimaced as he watch them descend, pinioning his hand between the smooth leather and the coarse concrete floor.

A smile played across her thin crimson lips. She closed her eyes and rose from the heels, placing the full weight of her body on the balls of her feet, and thus on the hands of the submissive male. Years of Yoga imbued her with balance, strength and concentration, and her body slowly rotated, grinding the hands beneath her feet. "Yes, today is the Matriarchal Birthday, when the males of the house honor the Goddess. I have a special game planned for today; something I think will please Grand-Mum."

She stepped away from the whimpering male and walked to the wall to retrieve a collar and leash. The heavy, leather posture collar was fastened to his neck and she jerked on the leash bringing him to a 'kneel-up' position. "Let's announce your coming, shall we?" she teased. Her fingers attacked his nipples, pulling and twisting on the tender buds until she'd achieved the look and shape she desired, then she attached the nipple clamps, each holding two silver bells. Her crop lashed out, painting a red steak across his ass, "Jiggle!"

The hapless male jerked his chest and shoulders, setting the bells to twinkling to the delight of his horrific Mistress and step-daughter.

She lashed out again with the crop, not because he'd been disobedient, but because she could – and it pleased her to do so. "Ah, twinkling titty bells," she laughed, "next to the cries and wails of males, one of my favorite sounds." Her wrist snapped at the lead, jerking him back down to his hands and knees. "Let's go, bitch, time to get this party started, and keep those bells ringing." She led him out the cell door, barely breaking her stride as she plucked a long dressage whip from the wall on the way out.

Margeaux de Kranow surveyed the scene before her. She reposed on one end of a long room, on an elevated dais in an elegantly carved mahogany chair finished in a rich damask. Her stylish Chanel suit was cut to fit her petite frame. Black kid gloves covered her arms and stylish black pumps adorned her feet. At eighty-three years of age her hair had long turned to silver, but her black eyes were alive as ever, missing nothing.

Poised in back of her throne, on the left and right, were her sissy maid attendants, Fifi and Chloe. Each sissy maid was attired in her formal serving uniform, a short black and white maid's dress, the skirts held almost horizontal by billowing petticoats. Black, fishnet, seamed stockings enclosed their legs and their feet were shod in gleaming six-inch stilettos that locked around each ankle. They wore elbow-length, white, lace gloves and kept their hands clasped behind their back until someone approached their Mistress, at which time each maid would grasp their skirt and execute a deep curtsey to honor the approaching guest.

They were kept busy, as the receiving line was quite long. Friends, guests and special invitees all queued up to pay their respects to the reigning Matriarch and Dominatrix of the clan. It was an annual event, repeated for generations of dominant de Kranow women who ruled the Dominant's Guild.

The room was alive with activity, and Margeaux's handmaidens were kept busy as they curtseyed and accepted the proffered birthday gifts from each visitor. At the end of the room was an elegant buffet, staffed by yet another group of male sissy maids. Chairs, in three elevations to provide unobstructed views for the assembled guests, lined both sides of the long room.

In the center of the room was the games area, today's activities designed and hosted by Margeaux's favorite, and most wicked grand-daughter, Audra. After her mother, Catherine, Audra was next in line to rule the dynasty. Margeaux smiled as she waited for the next guest to approach. *The dynasty is secure, Catherine and Audra are worthy successors, and there is never a shortage of men willing to submit to Feminine Authority.*

The sissy maid handmaidens went about their duties: curtseying, smiling, accepting gifts and arranging them on the reception table. They warily eyed the gaming area, thankful their status saved them from the impending agony that others would endure for the amusement of the assembled throng.

Audra's creation was simple, elegant and artistic, and would tax the game participants to the extreme. Three gleaming wooden beams ran parallel down the center of the room. The beams were six inches wide, smooth from hours of hand-sanding by sissy maids, and sealed and polished to a high sheen. But the most menacing aspect was the multitude of phalluses that jutted ominously from the long expanse of wood. Fourteen cocks, hand carved from a variety of exotic woods, were spaced equidistant along the length of each beam. They were graduated in size, from short and narrow, to monsters of hideous length and girth that resided at the ends of the beams that faced Margeaux's throne.

The sissy maids could only imagine the horrors that awaited today's gamers, and counted themselves lucky to be permanently chastised handmaidens. Chloe curtsied deeply as Mistress Catherine de Kranow and her lover, Andre, approached the dais.

Andre bowed and kissed Margeaux's gloved hand.

Margeaux smiled, her octogenarian eyes alive with fire, "Surely you can do better than that."

Andre cast a bemused look at Catherine, "Ah, the women in my life." He turned back to Margeaux, his lips taking hers in a smoldering kiss. As her tongue snaked into his mouth, his hand found her breast and squeezed it gently, but firmly. He felt her stiffen at his touch; the de Kranow women were extremely sensual. *Will Catherine be as sexual in her later years?* As the resident Alpha male Andre was a highly prized commodity in the household. While de Kranow women dominated men, had ruled over them for many generations, they always valued the true Alpha male and kept one or two in Court. Andre had indeed bedded all three of the current line, each generation taxing him in different, albeit pleasurable and stimulating ways.

Andre broke the kiss, bowed and kissed her hand again, a sign of respect and appreciation.

Margeaux smiled approvingly, "He's the best we've ever had, a true stallion." She reached out and felt Andre's crotch, approvingly noting his stiff member. "He rises to every occasion."

Catherine nodded, "He *is* special. Shall I send him to you this evening?"

"Yes," Margeaux replied, "but early. I'm sure he'll be able to meet his other obligations when I'm through with him."

Andre and Catherine bowed to their Matriarch, and walked hand-in-hand to join the other guests.

Audra led slave number 19 through the halls, pleased at the way he struggled to keep up, crawling on his hands and knees and shaking his upper body to keep his tittie bells ringing. She stopped at an alcove in the hallway.

The alcove held a sissy maid perched on her six inch stilettos and precariously balanced on a white marbled pedestal eighteen inches tall and twelve inches in diameter. The sissy maid was attired in the same uniform as Margeaux's handmaids.

Audra reached up and removed the chains from the sides of the alcove to the collar that was affixed to the sissy maid's neck. "Down!"

The sissy maid cautiously and silently stepped down from the pedestal.

"Aren't you two a pair?" mocked Audra, "my step-daddy slave and sissy maid step-brother. Don't recognize your own son? Hmm, probably not, especially since we've let *her* hair grow, started the hormone treatments – oh, and of course, those huge breasts we gave her." She cut the air with the Dressage whip, laughing as the two submissives flinched at both her action and the dreaded sound of the whip slicing the air. "We renamed him too; *your* Jack is now *our* Jacki." She kicked him in the fleshy part of the thigh, "And you, shit-for-brains, you're just slave 19." She poked the whip at her kneeling step-father, "I bet this was never on your radar when you married mother. You and sissy boy here were probably happy as pigs in shit to marry a beautiful woman who had a hot young daughter. Joke's on you boys, it didn't take long for mother to gain control of your assets – and then you." She paused, noting the stillness in the hallway. Her hand lashed out, the Dressage whip leaving a nasty welt on slave 19's back. "I don't hear my pretty bells!" She hit him again, "Where's my tittie music?" She smiled as the kneeling slave furiously shook his breasts. "Better."

She held the whip under his chin, forcing him to

look up. "Take a look at your son; been a few months since you've seen her. She's now my own sissy hand maid; much more useful that way than as a step-brother." Audra pointed the whip at the sissy maid, "Watch this daddy. OVER!"

At the command 'over' the sissy maid bent at the waist and lifted her dress and petticoats. Her ass was bare, no panties, and delicately framed by a sexy black garter belt and the black lace tops of her stockings.

Audra playfully tapped her whip against the bare, creamy skin. "A little bare, don't you think? Let's give her some color." She raised her hand and flicked the whip, the dreadful whooshing sound ending in a 'thwack' against the sissy maid's pink flesh.

Immediately after the blow, the sissy maid began wiggling her bottom. "Look at that," Audra laughed, "she's begging for more." Audra delivered another stroke of the whip, eliciting more bottom-wiggling from her victim. "She's been trained to do that; she'll wiggle that saucy ass after each stroke, begging me for yet another, until I tire of our little game. How's that daddy? Your son didn't take over the business as you'd hoped. Mother and I took that, and your son's destiny is to be my personal sissy maid slut while you languish as a slave in your cell."

The sissy maid was whipped four more times before Audra commanded, "Up! OK, my bitches, it's showtime." Mistress Audra led her charges forward, to their fates.

Margeaux extended her gloved right hand, her palm turned up and thumb and forefinger nearly touching. Sissy maid Fifi responded immediately, inserting a cigarette into a twelve inch gleaming black cigarette holder adorned with Swarovski crystals. Fifi gently placed the holder in Mistress's hand while Chloe stood ready with a lighter. Margeaux smoked while Chloe knelt at her side, holding a large and heavy crystal ashtray in her outstretched palm.

The throng of well wishers had diminished, and everyone was enjoying the lavish food and drink served by a bevy of attentive and submissive sissy maids.

Mistress Margeaux blew a contemptuous stream of smoke into Chole's face and gazed among the crowd. She waved her cigarette holder like a wand, the embedded crystals catching and reflecting the light into an ethereal trail. "And where is my darling Granddaughter?"

The lights dimmed, not to darkness, but for a dramatic effect. A red spot light flooded the entrance as the heavy wooden doors at the end of the room opened easily and silently on their hinges.

"I am here, Grandmother, to honor you on this most glorious of days." Audra stepped into the light, pulling the leashes of her servile minions, slave 19 crawling and Jacki teetering on stilettos. She knew the power of dramatic effects, both as entertainment value to the assembled Dominants, and to spark terror of the impending events into the hearts of the submissives in attendance.

Audra stopped and removed her slave's leashes, casting them to the side of the room where an awaiting sissy maid quickly scooped them up. She walked behind the two submissives and used her whip to prod them forward. "Go, and pay your respects."

They proceeded up the long room, the red spot light following their every move. Audra's and Jacki's stilettos clicked on the smooth and polished parquet floor, while slave 19 shuffled along on his hands and knees to the twinkling of his tittie bells.

Hushed conversations followed them up the room:

"The one crawling is Catherine's husband."
"She never divorced him, but took everything."
"And the sissy maid is his son?"
"Oh yes, his, but not Catherine's. She'd never give birth to a creature like that. Catherine and Audra enslaved both males."

When they reached the dais Jacki curtseyed and slave 19 crawled to the Margeaux's feet. The crowd nodded and murmured appreciatively as Catherine looked on, proud of her daughter's handling of her husband and step son. The carefully choreographed activities were set to begin.

Margeaux raised her exquisite high-heeled pump, exposing the sole to slave 19 who dutifully extended his tongue and lavished his love on Mistress's shoe. She barely acknowledged this act, confident that when a lady's shoe was offered to a competent slave natural training instincts would take over: see a shoe, lick it clean, a lesson literally beaten into them.

A snap of her gloved fingers summoned Jacki forward, and Jacki approached and curtseyed.

Margeaux spread her gloved hands wide, "This is Jacki, my sissy maid grandson, not by birth of course, but still a delightful creature, don't you think?"

The room burst into applause and Jacki curtseyed to acknowledge their compliment.

"Bend over girl," Margeaux commanded.

Jacki complied, placing her hands behind her back and bending forward at the waist.

Margeaux reached forward and pulled the sissy maid's dress down, exposing a pair of impressive 44DD breasts. "Show everyone how I spoil my girls."

Jacki spun on her heels, faced the crowd, bent forward and jiggled her breasts in the most shameless manner. The crowd erupted into laughter and applause.

Margeaux raised her hand and stilled the crowd. "When Audra left for college we sent Jacki with her. Not to be educated, academics are much too taxing for a sissy maid. No, our delicate little Jacki spent her college years as the house girl at Audra's sorority house. When Audra graduated I gave her a sports car, and to reward Jacki's service for those years of toil and humiliation," Margeaux paused, "we gave her those wondrous titties."

Once more the crowd applauded and Jacki shook her titties, evoking even louder applause and laughter.

Margeaux uncrossed her legs and offered her other shoe sole to slave 19. She didn't bother to look down, confident that the creature would go about its shoe licking duty until instructed otherwise. "And now my lovely Granddaughter will host today's games."

Audra bowed to the crowd and stepped onto the dais, embraced Margeaux on both cheeks, and turned to face the crowd. "Thank you, we are here today to honor the Grand Matriarch of The Dominant's Guild. In her honor," she pointed to the three wooden beams, "and for your entertainment, I have devised a new game, a test of slave endurance." She clapped her hands and three slaves were ushered into the room.

The slaves were naked and their bodies oiled, they glistened in the room's diffused lighting. Their nipples had been pierced by large golden rings. Most notable, besides the nudity, was their complete lack of hair, their bodies and heads were shaved, even their eyebrows were gone and their eyelashes plucked out.

Two of the slaves were of average height, while the third was shorter and certainly younger. All were of average build; the slave's life of constant work and limited food, limited their ability to develop muscular bodies.

Audra snapped her fingers at Jacki, a non-verbal command to follow, and Mistress and sissy maid left the dais and walked to the slave trio.

"These slaves," Audra said as she approached her quarry, "were selected for today's event because of their recent poor performance. They will suffer today, both physically and mentally, for your amusement." The crowd clapped; the Matriarchal Birthday was always a celebration that involved some sort of slave contest; traditions were highly valued by The Guild.

Audra spun on one of her wicked heels and slowly walked the length of one of the wooden beams. Her hand lovingly caressed each intricately carved wooden phallus. "Today's game is Self-Impalement. Of course it would be easy for us to simply tie the creatures down," she glared over her shoulder at the slaves, "and fuck their sissy asses raw!" She quickly took on a softer tone, her words sweet and tender, "But how much more exquisite it is to make them commit the act themselves, to force their puckered openings over these shafts." The crowd nodded their approval as they watched Audra caress the largest of the wooden phalluses, her hand unable to fully grasp it.

"Of course it will be easy, at first, but as they get nearer the end the task becomes," Audra smiled as she gripped the largest phallus, "quite formidable. It's a race; first one to the end wins. And what does the winner get?" She laughed and shrugged her shoulders, "Nothing! The losers get punished, a severe caning and whipping with the last-place finisher receiving extensive punishment."

The crowd cheered, a slave game and a punishment session, today would be truly memorable.

"There are some refinements," Audra said. "At the base of each wooden cock are pressure and temperature sensors. These will record the performance of each slave's impalement. Each slave must take it all, settle that sissy ass to the beam and squeeze tight. He can only move to the next cock when he gets a light and a beep which signify a full and successful impalement." Audra turned and pointed to Jacki, "My sissy slut will demonstrate."

Audra positioned Jacki at the beginning of the center wooden beam and ordered, "Remove your dress." Jacki disrobed while Audra further explained, "This one has been pre-lubed for the demonstration. Our slut will start with the smallest one and work her way to the end. There are red and green lights between each set of wooden cocks. When the game starts, all lights will turn to red. Each slave will only be able to move to the next cock when the light goes green. The green lights are connected to the pressure and temperature sensors, so our slaves will have to sink that cock deep into their ass and squeeze it hard to get the go-ahead to move to the next."

Jacki stood at the end of the beam. She'd removed her maid's dress and wore only a garter belt, stockings and stilettos. Her large breasts were now prominently on display, their size made more pronounced by the tiny metal chastity that enclosed her cock.

Audra stood before her sissy maid and slapped the enormous tits, delighting the crowd as the fleshy globes bounced back and forth between her hands. When her fingers pinched Jacki's nipples the sissy maid swooned and went weak in the knees.

"What a slut!" someone yelled from the crowd.

"Yes," laughed Audra, "and we're about to see a true display of sluttiness." She reached down and flicked a switch carefully recessed into the beam and a series of red lights illuminated between each wooden cock. Audra slapped Jacki's ass sending the teetering sissy forward on her high heels. "Fuck those cocks, bitch!"

To the crowd's cheers of 'Fuck those cocks, bitch' Jacki straddled the beam and positioned her sissi pussi over the first, and smallest, phallus. It easily slid in and Jacki settled fully onto the beam, wiggling her bottom to make full contact. It took only a few seconds and everyone heard a 'BEEP' and the red light went out and a green light illuminated.

In game show host style Audra mocked, "And now, on to cock number two!"

Once more the crowd joined in, cheering Jacki on with chants of: "Fuck that cock, bitch!" and "Cock number two!"

Jacki located the second cock at her entrance and then slid down, giving a wiggle or two on the way. Several in the crowd smiled as they watched the impaled sissy slut clench her buttocks. When the green light came on, Jacki rose and proceeded to cock number three.

As the sissy made her way down the line of cocks Audra walked to the three slaves who would participate in the upcoming game. "Don't be fooled, it's not as easy as she's making it look." Audra turned to watch Jacki settle on the seventh cock, to the catcalls of the crowd. Audra walked behind the three slaves and barked "Over!" As trained, they all bent at the waist. One by one, Mistress Audra used her hands to spread their buttocks. "No, I'm afraid that the three of you are going to have significantly more trouble than my slut Jacki. She was well used during my college days: my sorority sisters who wanted to experiment with strap-ons, boyfriends, gay friends, everyone had a piece of her over the years. But you my babies, I know you've not had that much experience." Audra's hand slapped the ass of the smallest and youngest of the slaves. "What about you, ever had anything up there."

The slave literally shook with fear, "N – n – no, Mistress, never, please, I can-"

"A virgin!" Audra yelled, "we have a virgin today."

The crowd turned their attention from Jacki, who'd only just risen from cock number twelve. "A virgin." "Fresh meat." "This'll be the one to watch."

Audra grabbed the virgin's head and pointed it toward Jacki as the sissy positioned herself over cock thirteen. "Watch this," Audra whispered in the trembling slave's ear.

Jacki slowly descended, and then quickly rose. She took a deep breath and descended again, rotating her hips as the huge wooden phallus poked at her opening.

Audra's fingers caressed the virgin's nipples as she whispered, "She's getting it all lined up, positioning is sooo critical at this stage."

The virgin slave whimpered, making Audra smile. "See how she's going slower now, even though she's been stretched by all those other cocks, these last ones are so big." Audra thought the slave might faint, but she continued her teasing torment. "You'll need to breathe and relax, it will feel so good when it makes its way through that ring of muscles and goes all the way in. Mmmmm, you'll love the way it fills you up. A big cock up your ass." She felt the slave's legs go weak.

"No, oh god, please no, I can't, I never-"

Audra viciously pinched his nipple, bringing him back to reality. "You will, bitch! You'll ride those cocks and entertain my guests. Believe me; the punishments of not doing it will be much more horrible." They both watched as Jacki rose and moved to the last cock. "See, it can be done. Of course my sissy Jacki is a pro, a well-trained ass slut. Don't worry; we'll make one of you as well."

The crowed voiced an appreciative 'Ahhh' as Jacki worked her ass over and down the last gargantuan phallus. Her face contorted into a grimace as she forced herself all the way down and squeezed, giving the wooden cock every last ounce of her ass love. The crowd erupted into applause and cheers as the beep sounded and the light turned green. Jacki slowly rose from the cock, gingerly lifting her ass off, before turning to the crowd and executing a curtsey on shaky legs.

"That, ladies and gentlemen, is how it will be done," Audra announced. "One slave will win and go back to his daily life as a slave, perhaps with a sore ass, but no worse for wear. The remaining slaves will be punished, the last-place finisher receiving the worst of it."

The young virgin slave panicked, broke free from Audra, and ran the length of the room towards Mistress Margeaux. "No, no, please, I can't do it; I've never done that, the pain, I…"

He fell in a sobbing heap at Margeaux's feet.

Fifi and Chloe quickly closed on the crying slave, preventing him from reaching their Mistress.

"Stand up this impudent slave," Margeaux commanded. "Pin his tits and bring me my whip." She snapped her fingers, pointed beside her chair and kicked away slave 19, *I'll deal with him later*.

The shoe licking slave quickly took a kneeling position beside Mistress's chair, glad to give his sore tongue a rest, and giving thanks that he wasn't going to be the center of her attention for the next few minutes.

Fifi hoisted the young slave to his feet while Chloe retrieved Margeaux's vicious Dressage whip.

"Do both tits," Margeaux ordered. "I'll not tolerate such disobedience from slaves. You WILL ride those cocks. Likely you'll lose, but I guarantee a visit to hell if you dare disobey." As she talked, Chloe methodically placed clothespins on the slave's nipples and tits.

The crowd had moved forward, not wanting to miss a chance to see their Matriarch in action. They watched as Fifi and Chloe each took one of the slave's outstretched arms and positioned him facing Mistress Margeaux.

"I've been taking males in hand for seven decades," Margeaux held the whip in her hand, testing its balance and motioning for Fifi and Chloe to move the slave to the left. "You're going to learn a lesson, a painful one, about obedience." She flicked her wrist and the Dresage whip cut the air, its vicious end snapping a clothespin from the sissy virgin's left tit. The sissy howled and Margeaux smiled and closed her eyes, "The screams of males in pain, my darling, you'll howl arias of agony this day." She opened her eyes, fixing them on the next target, and flicked another clothespin from the tender flesh.

The slave struggled, but Fifi and Chloe held him tight, thankful his outstretched arms put them well out of the way of the evil whip.

Margeaux held the whip in both hands, her right hand gripping the black, leather-wrapped handle with a silver pommel, while her left hand, gloved in black leather, stroked the supple shaft. "Can you imagine how many I've whipped over the years? Easily hundreds; this whip has tasted the flesh of many slaves. It can sting, cut, even remove the flesh." She held the whip at arm's length, resting the tip on a clothespin on the slave's right nipple, marking her target, "This one next, I think."

The sissy didn't even get a chance to plead before her wrist flicked and the whip found its target, the clothespin flying across the room and the sissy screaming.

"Next," Margeaux teased, and sent another clothespin flying.

Someone in the crowd offered, "Three in a row please, my Lady."

Margeaux smiled, and quickly dispatched three clothespins, the sissy writhing in pain as each was ripped from his body by the lightning-fast application of her whip.

"You – think," she said, punctuating each word with a strike of her whip, "that because I'm old, I've lost skills?" Her eyes judged the distance to her next targets, "But – I've – more – than – enough – skills – to – deal – with – the – likes – of – you!"

Her target was wailing and gasping, torrents of pain running through him. Were it not for Fifi and Chloe's assistance he would have collapsed.

Margeaux fixed her last target, teasingly tapping it with her whip, delighting in the way he flinched at each tap. "Open your eyes, I want you to watch."

The slave opened his eyes, watching in terror as Margeaux toyed with the clothespin.

"You must beg me to remove it, to relieve your torment. Beg for my whip." Margeaux's tone was soft, motherly.

The slave sobbed, "Please Mistress, let me feel your whip one last time, please Mistress." His eyes grew wide as he watched her hand go back and saw the whip fly forward only stop short of its mark.

The crowd laughed as they watched Margeaux toy with her prey, drawing out the last strike. Just as he breathed his sigh of relief she lashed out, the whip exploding on his flesh and the clothespin clattering to the floor.

Margeaux held out the whip to Chloe, who released her hold on the slave, curtseyed, and gently took the whip from her Mistress. The crowd applauded and Margeaux acknowledged them with a wave of her hand. "And now," she said, "perhaps the games many commence. Three on his tongue," she pointed to the slave, "it may shut him up a bit as he attempts to ride the cocks."

The slave squirmed to no avail as Chloe and Fifi

clipped three clothespins to his tongue. The two sissy maids escorted him back to his slave companions, who'd watched the events in horror.

"And now," Audra bowed to Margeaux, "in your honor M'Lady, these slaves will compete to see who can ride the cocks the quickest." She snapped her fingers and three sissy maids minced in on their stilettos and stood by each wooden beam. Each maid wore latex gloves and carried unmarked tubes.

"These sissy maids will prepare the cocks for you, giving them heavy coats of lubricant."

The naked slaves breathed a collective sigh of relief; at least they wouldn't be impaling themselves on dry wood.

Audra noted their looks; she'd planned on exactly that moment of slight relief, all the better to now destroy any signs of hope. "It won't be that easy my unfortunate sluts." She pointed to the sissy maids who were working their way down the beams, lubing each cock, and using one of the three different tubes of lube each time. "Two of those tubes contain ordinary lube, but one of the tubes contains a deep heating balm." She laughed as she watched the color drain from their faces. "Yes, I suggest that when you encounter one of those cocks you get it over with quickly, get on, get down and get off. The longer you linger…"

"You," Audra pointed to the virgin sissy with the clothespins on his tongue and the drool running down his chin, "you take the middle position." She held up a long thin chain with clips at each end, "One last ingredient to make it – interesting."

Audra walked to one of the slaves on the outside

and clipped one end of the chain to the ring on his outside nipple. She ran the chain through his inside nipple ring, and then through the nipple rings on the inside slave, through the inside nipple ring on the other outside slave and finally clipping it to his own outside ring. "There now, all joined as one, aren't we? It's a race, remember, but don't move to the next cock until you get the beep and the green light indicating you've fully impaled yourself." She moved to the center slave, "It's obvious you're not as experienced in these matters as your competitors, but I *strongly* recommend you do your best to keep up." She grabbed the chain running the slave's nipple rings and pulled it tight, delighting in how the slave's eyes grew wide with fear as he watched his nipples distend. "What a delightful conundrum, pain up here, or down there." She dropped the chain, "Fuck yourself, deeply and quickly, because these two," she pointed to the slaves to her left and right, "won't be waiting for you."

Audra saw that the last cocks were being lubed. She quickly hung signs around the neck of each of the slaves, the center slave was number '3', the one to the left '24', and the one on the right was '17'. "It seems we are ready." She took a glass of Champagne from a sissy maid who was making the rounds with a large tray of glasses, and raised her glass, "To Lady Margeaux, our supreme and much beloved Matriarch, on this most glorious day of her birth, long life and many slaves, to Lady Margeaux."

The room echoed with a chorus of "To Lady Margeaux."

Margeaux stood, "Thank you all for coming. It won't be long before I yield my place to my daughter Catherine, but each year I see the Guild grow stronger, with new members," she cast a wicked smile at the three slaves, "and with new submissives." She raised her own glass, "To the Guild."

A second time the room reverberated with, "To the guild."

Margeaux reposed in her chair and crossed her legs. She lifted her Champagne glass in Audra's direction, "And now, a little entertainment."

The lights dimmed, to be replaced by an array of spotlights highlighting each beam. The slaves would truly be performing, a spectacle of self impalement for the amusement of their assembled Mistresses.

Audra stalked behind the terrified trio, "When I say "GO" you straddle the beam and begin. Do not skip a cock, fuck them all, miss one and you lose. Wait for the green light and the beep before you proceed to the next cock. If you don't get a green light and beep – well – you're simply not fucking yourself hard enough. Move down the line without a green light, and you lose. First one to the end, who successfully fucks all the cocks wins – nothing!"

Audra paused to whisper in number 3's ear, "Work fast, keep up. Mind you, this crowd wouldn't mind seeing your nipples ripped off, but it would be messy. Better to simply abuse that lovely virgin ass for us."

She stepped back to get a good view of the slaves' asses and the first lubed phallus. "Ready – Set – GO!"

The trio of slaves performed exactly as Audra

would have imagined, she could read submissive males, their temperaments, their reactions to stimuli, they held no surprises for her. Number 3 approached the first phallus, carefully positioning his hole over the device, flinching as his tender puckered opening made first contact. By contrast, the slaves to either side of him, grabbed their ass cheeks, spread themselves wide and quickly settled on the cocks. Even still, when they both got the audible beep and the green light, they rose delicately, and breathed a sigh of relief. *By six they'll be struggling, and on the last three we'll all get a good show.*

The virgin sissy, number 3, settled cautiously onto his phallus, even as his compatriots were positioning themselves for number two. The slack was coming out of the nipple chains. Audra watched as number 3 put his full weight on the beam, waiting for the light to change from red to green. *He's not going to make it, those lovely golden nipple rings are going to be ripped from his smooth and hairless chest. He'll be hauled off the beam and punished.*

The two outside slaves had moved on, one firmly settled on cock three as the other was beginning his self-impalement. The one on the left was halfway down when he felt the difference; this cock was not so much smooth and slick as it was greasy, the deep-heating balm. Audra noticed his pause and took delight in his fear and suffering. "All the cocks! And all the way down!" she barked.

The crowd roared with laughter as his body shook as he slid down the shaft, his ass cheeks clenching to activate the pressure sensors."Grip that cock," someone yelled. "Show us some submissive ass love," said another.

The other outside slave looked over in horror, thankful he was spared the agony, but dreading his fuck procession up the beam, knowing the same contaminated cocks awaited him.

Audra smiled, it would be a few seconds before the onslaught of the heating balm hit home. "Best thing to do is put more cocks with lube in that ass, dilute that foul shit," she yelled. "Fuck that ass," she taunted, "and you'll feel so much better."

When he got the signal to move the slave came off the cock like a rocket, eliciting howls of laughter from the crowd. He quickly moved to cock four, spread his ass cheeks, now burning with pain, and dropped quickly on the cock, its entry forcing a gasp from his lips.

Margeaux was enjoying the show; Audra was always creative in devising new games and slave entertainments. She glanced over at Jacki and her son-in-law slave 19, and snapped her fingers, "Service my girls."

Fifi and Chloe jumped up and down on their stilettos and clapped their hands. Then both offered deep curtsies to Mistress Margeaux. As the sissy hand maidens bent at the waist and lifted their dresses and petticoats, Jacki and slave 19 crawled forward on their hands and knees, one kneeling behind each of Margeaux's hand maidens.

Fifi and Chloe reached behind and spread their bottoms as Jacki and slave 19 licked at the hand maiden's rosebuds. Chloe's hand pulled Jacki's head deeper in the cleft of the sissy maid's bottom. "Deeper, slut!" Chloe ordered. Permanently chastised sissy maids such as Fifi and Chloe found few sexual pleasures, so when one was given an opportunity to experience a blissful ass-licking, one took every opportunity to enjoy it to the fullest.

Margeaux smiled approvingly, how heartwarming

it was for her to see her son-in-law on his knees, his tongue lavishing all its affections on a simpering sissy maid's ass, as his very own son did the same. *It's the lot of some males, they're born to serve, to suffer and endure.*

The action on the beams was reaching a critical point. The second outside slave had found his own cock coated with heating balm and was screaming as the crowd jeered. The outside slaves were on cocks five and six, while their inexperienced center victim was on cock number three.

The nipple chain was growing tighter, slave 3's nipples pulled taut. Audra reached out with her whip and tapped the chain. "I'd hurry if I were you," she teased.

Slave 3 only whimpered, but quickly came off the cock when the green light flashed. Just as he started to settle on cock four he felt the difference. He quickly stood and looked around, panic in his eyes. A chant of, "Down, down, fuck the cock, down, down, fuck the cock," filled the room. He stood, shaking, fearful, his body now pulled slightly forward by the chains connecting his nipples to the two slaves moving ahead of him.

Audra lashed out with her Dressage whip, cutting a crimson stripe across his thigh, "Down," she ordered, "on the cock."

His knees bent as he slowly lowered onto the fiery invader. This one was bigger, not a good thing as this was the cock he desperately need to get on and off of in a hurry. He was sobbing as he wiggled in an attempt to push it past that tight ring of muscle in his anus. He was beginning to feel the burning – and it wasn't even inside. His focus on the anal intruder distracted him from the pain and impending horror about to be inflicted on his nipples.

His competitors were well ahead of him, their own nipples now enduring the strain of the chain as well. Audra lightly tapped the chain with her whip, testing the chain, judging the distance. *The next one, yes, the next one should probably do it.*

It happened when the slave on the right rose from cock six and proceeded to number seven. There was no discernable noise, not from the ring tearing away from the nipple. The room's ambient noise, people talking, cheering the slaves on, the clinking of glasses all drowned out the sound of tearing flesh. The cry of the slave was another matter; it was a shriek that pierced the air, a forlorn wail drawing everyone's attention.

Slave number 3 grabbed at his chest, crimson rivulets cascading from his fingers.

It was clear to the crowd that this slave's day was done; he was surely the loser, and within seconds the other nipple ring would be yanked out. Indeed, almost as if on cue, the panic-stricken slave watched and reeled in pain as the chain made its last move forward, taking the golden ring with it and leaving the slave behind.

He stood, naked, his hands clutched to his chest. A tall, red-headed Dominant, dressed in leather and stiletto boots walked to him and rudely pulled his hands away from his chest. "Let's cleanse the wound, shall we?" she taunted. The slave's screams mixed with the crowd's laughter as she slowly poured a glass of vodka over the bleeding nipples.

Audra motioned for two naked male slaves to come forward. "Take this loser and tie him to the cross," she commanded. The two male slaves walked number 3 to the end of the room and bound him to a punishment cross.

All attention was now focused on the two remaining slaves. As Audra had predicted, the last three cocks were the hardest for the slaves and the most entertaining for the crowd. The last cock, the largest, was coated with cool, soothing lubricant. The next-to-last cock, however, was coated with the dreaded heating balm.

Slave 24 was working to seat himself fully on cock twelve, as slave 17 was spreading his ass to open himself for cock thirteen. As 17 descended he felt the difference and knew his only salvation was to get on and off this one quickly and on to the final cock, which hopefully contained only lubricant. The problem was that these last cocks were hideously large. They would have probably been too large for the slave to accommodate, had he not been stretching himself out from each previous self-fuck. He adjusted his posture and his breathing, used every slave ass-fuck trick he knew to get the monster inside him. Slowly he wiggled his way down, letting his full weight settle to the beam. In actuality, had it not been a humiliating competition, had the cocks not have been coated with the tortuous heating balm, it may have felt nice to feel so filled. Most male slaves were rigorously trained to take their sexual pleasure in this fashion.

He grimaced as the light illuminated and he rose from the cock. Slave 17 turned to see his competitor well behind him. Feeling that his victory was now well in-hand, slave 17 looked up to Mistress Margeaux and deeply bowed as he lowered himself onto the final cock.

Margeax returned his oblation with her own nod of approval and smiled as she watched the huge wooden phallus disappear into his flesh. She looked to see Chloe and Fifi squealing as their asses were tongue worshipped.

When slave 17 rose from his final cock he dropped to his knees, bringing his head to the ground. Audra walked forward and unclipped the chain from his nipple rings and kicked him forward. He crawled to the feet of Mistress Margeaux and kissed the toe of her shoe.

"I name you the winner of today's contest," Margeaux announced, and the crowd cheered.

"This slave will be returned to his cage to rest," Audra said. "These other two, the losers, will be available for public punishment. The last place finisher," she pointed to slave number 3, bound to the cross at the end of the room, "will serve twelve hours of public punishment. The second place finisher," she pointed to slave 24, who was being secured to a spanking horse, "will serve six hours of public punishment." Some of the crowd were already selecting various paddles, crops and whips, and milling around the unfortunate slaves.

Catherine and Andre joined Audra and Margeaux on the dais. "One last ceremonial function to perform," Margeaux said. She clapped her hands, "Enough ass licking you sluts!"

Jacki and slave 19 immediately backed away from the asses that had consumed their faces, and Chloe and Fifi turned and curtsied their thanks to their Mistress.

"Each year, on my birthday" Margeaux explained, "we select a group of slaves who have exhibited outstanding performance. They are allowed an ejaculation, a genuine orgasm, *if* they can achieve one. If not, they may at least derive some pleasure from the trying."

Audra snapped her fingers at a sissy maid attending the door. The maid opened the door and ushered in ten naked males who were paraded before the dais.

"These are this year's fortunate slaves, chosen by a committee of the Guild. As in years past, their," Marge-ax paused and smiled, "reward shall be administered by my servile step son, known now only as slave 19."

Audra flicked her whip, striping the haunches of slave 19 and driving him forward, crawling to the line of slaves. The slaves eagerly queued up, more than ready to have their cocks sucked and for the chance to enjoy a real orgasm and ejaculation.

Margeaux beamed as she watched her son-in-law's mouth fill with cock after cock, the slaves grabbing his bald head and pulling it as they fucked his face. Slave cum and drool coated his chin and she smiled with satisfaction as she noted that some of the slaves were still able to ejaculate. "If any of you can still get hard after the cock sucking, you may fuck the slut's ass," Margaeux said.

The slaves eagerly bowed their thanks to their Mistress, who gleefully noted some of the slaves starting to rise to the occasion.

The Guild photographer took commemorative photographs of Margeaux, Catherine and Audra, as guests enjoyed food and drink to the cries and wails of the slaves on the cross and the horse.

Audra stood back to survey the scene, the ornate room, resplendent guests, expensive food and drink, and naked slaves. She watched her sissy maid step brother, Jacki, back in maid livery; carrying a tray of drinks. Slave 19 was now servicing two slaves at a time, both his orifices filled with cocks too long denied and eager for a chance at pleasure before being locked up for who knew how long.

Audra ran her hand over the back of Margeaux's

regal chair. *Soon it will be mother who sits on this chair, and someday it will be my time.* She bent down to place a loving kiss on Margeaux's cheek. "It's been a wonderful day Grandmother, Happy Birthday."

END

He came face to face with the clear acrylic heel, locking eyes with the face of the male trapped inside. "There's…there's somebody in there."

She laughed; for a writer, an *intellectual*, he seemed a bit slow. "Men are heels, in this case…literally."

His hand rubbed the smooth surface, "They're alive." The heels were clear acrylic, six feet tall, and shaped like a classic spike heel. Inside was a hairless male, facing forward toward the shoe's sole, somehow crammed in so he filled the heel and was completely immobile.

"Of course they're alive; imagine how they'd begin to smell if they were dead. And you can torment the live ones; it is, after all, another interactive exhibit."

PERFORMANCE ART

This time there were four of them; they worked slowly and methodically, occasionally positioning him for better access and ignoring his pleas and moans as they chatted about fashion, restaurants and films. He screamed, "My name is Simon Warton. I'm a reporter for Art Edge magazine. You have to help me!" Or at least that's what his mind told him to say. To his ears it sounded like "mghph gghhffp gghhpphh mnmngfh..."

TWO DAYS Earlier...

"*I*m Elizabeth Stansbury," she extended a hand enclosed in a brown kidskin leather glove.

"Simon Warton, Art Edge magazine, very pleased to make your acquaintance." Her handshake was firm; everything about her was – impressive? Imposing? In her designer four inch heels she stood at least three inches taller than his five-eight. Her rich and elegantly coiffed silver hair put her age in her late 50s or 60s, but her skin was still flawless, smooth and creamy, perfect makeup; he didn't see any lines indicating surgical enhancements. *Good genetics or high maintenance* he thought. A perfectly fitted Chanel suit emphasized a woman's shape, with curves that provoked more than a casual glance. It was her eyes that caught his attention: brown, with flecks of gold that caught the light. But - there was something about them: *not lifeless, but not giving anything away, haunting, yet mysterious.* "I'm anxious to have this opportunity to see your exhibit, it's all somewhat of a – mystery. I'm glad my publisher was able to arrange it."

She motioned her guest to sit as she poured coffee. "Debra is an old and dear friend, and when she called and asked if she could send you over I immediately agreed. Yes, the exhibit is very exclusive, open by special appointment and personal referrals only." Her eyes looked him over: reasonably fit, a thick head of curly hair and a handsome face. She smiled at the tufts of hair that peeked from his designer polo shirt and took note.

He saw her studied look; it gave him pause. "Is there something – wrong?"

She gracefully handed him the cup and saucer. "Nothing at all. Cream and sugar?"

His hand accepted the delicate china cup and saucer; the coffee was rich, much like his hostess and her surroundings. He thought about his editor, Debra Parker, *the fat cow, I should be editing Art Edge, what she knows about art wouldn't fill this cup.* "Uh – the exhibit - why such secrecy?"

Elizabeth sat back and crossed her legs, watching his eyes drawn to her shimmery ankles and the rustle of expensive stockings. She tented her fingers and her piercing eyes locked on his. "Not so much a secret as being – discreet, exclusive. The exhibit is not to everyone's taste."

"So, it's controversial? Like, Mapplethorpe?"

She slowly pulled off her gloves, one finger at a time, her eyes never leaving his. "Yes, it could be considered controversial," she pursed her lips, "it's performance art…of an erotic nature."

"Performance art? With live people?" He held out a small digital recorder, "May I take notes, put this on the record?"

She smiled, "Of course, everything on the record. I told Debra I'd be most accommodating to her number one reporter. I assured her she'd be *completely* satisfied."

"Great!" He moved the switch to 'on' and set the unit on the coffee table between them.

She poured herself coffee, added sugar and slowly stirred, the spoon never touching the cup.

Simon leaned forward, "A sexual nature? Erotica? People performing sex? Gay? Lesbian?"

"Dominance and submission." Her eyebrows arched, "Are you shocked?"

"You mean like whips and chains, leather, bondage, sex slaves?"

She smiled, her eyes taking on life. "More refined." She saw his excitement.

Her gracious reticence was beginning to get on his nerves. She claimed to be open, but he had to slowly pry each bit of information from her. *Women and their fucking games!* "Who are the artists?"

"The artists are all women, select artisans from my own private circle who I commissioned to do the various pieces of the exhibit."

"Really? All women…why?"

She leaned forward to place her coffee on the table. She was close enough for him to smell her Chanel perfume. *She's probably twice my age, but I'd do her, hell maybe a couple of times.*

"The reason I employ only women artists is the theme of the exhibit…Female Domination."

He chuckled, and failed to note her derision when he did. "You mean women in boots and leather corsets, stuff like that?"

"A stereotype, an iconic image more fit for television, movies, trashy novels and magazines," she huffed. She'd tolerate this creature, see this through to the end, she'd do it for her friendship with Debra.

"And my publisher, Debra, she knows about this?"

"She does, she recommended one of the artists."

He let out a low whistle. *Well, Debra, guess there's more to you than I thought.* "So, only women artists in the exhibit."

Elizabeth nodded, "And only women visitors and guests."

His surprise was obvious, "You mean men aren't allowed to visit the exhibit? It really is women only?"

"Men are the - subjects - of the exhibit. They are viewed by women, but no male guests or visitors have been permitted. You," she paused, enjoying the moment, "will be the first."

"No shit, I can't wait."

"Neither, my dear boy, can I."

"For security reasons, we won't use the main entrance. We'll use one of the maintenance access doors. I'll wait for you inside, and Caroline will prepare you." She pointed to a small, unlabeled door. "Go on, I'll meet you inside the exhibit."

He opened the door and went inside. A stunning young blond, her hair in a tight, severe bun, sat behind a nondescript desk. "Hello, I'm Simon – "

"Yes, I know who you are." She rose and approached him. Where Elizabeth had been dressed in fashionable elegance, her young assistant was the epitome of fetish couture. A tight black pencil skirt molded to her hips and thighs. Her crisp white blouse was partially unbuttoned to reveal the hint of a lacy bra and full breasts.

Now her, her I could do all night, and then some.

"Please remove your clothing; you may put it in that locker."

When she turned to point to the locker he looked instead at her black, seamed stockings and skyscraper, stiletto heels. "Excuse me?"

"Clothed males are NOT allowed in the exhibit hall."

"Wait, I don't think you understand. I'm a reporter, a writer, for Art Edge magazine. Ms Stansbury was going to give me a personally guided tour of the exhibit - for a story - for the magazine." Once more he found himself looking *up* at a woman. This one had to be six-three in her heels. *What the fuck is going on?*

"Ms Stansbury is on the other side of that door,"

Caroline pointed to a mahogany door, "waiting for you – a naked you. Please remove your clothing. Trust me, you will not shock or alarm any of *us*."

For a brief moment he felt fear - dread. He had the impulse to turn and leave, kiss off the assignment and go get drunk - and laid.

Caroline stood her ground, towering over him, her arms crossed over those magnificent breasts, her green eyes cutting a hole through his skull.

"Aw, what the hell, it's a story…right?" He pulled his shirt over his head and unbuckled his belt. "Anything for art, huh?"

For the first time the hint of a smile crossed Caroline's lips, "Yes, we must sacrifice - everything - for our art."

As promised, he found the regal and imposing Elizabeth Stansbury waiting for him in the Exhibit Hall foyer. The door closed behind him with a heavy thud and click, and out of instinct he tried the handle. Locked.

The clicking of Elizabeth's heels turned his attention back to her. She seemed oblivious to his nakedness. In her hand she held a collar and a leash. She held out the collar, "Put this on."

"Hey, Elizabeth - Ms Stansbury - I've had some kinky sex, ya know…but - "

"This isn't for your pleasure." Her tone was unyielding, "My guests don't expect to see *any* males, other than in the exhibits, so you must be properly presented and escorted. I'll NOT have my artistic theme compromised!"

He held up a conciliatory hand, "OK, OK, I'm here…so…yea…OK" He reluctantly fastened the collar around his neck. Before he'd even removed his hands from his neck she walked away, pulling the leash taut and jerking him forward.

"The exhibit runs for nine weeks." She led him through a hallway filled with paintings of women dominating men, and rows of padded benches. "We have other venues available to us if attendance and interest warrants. This is the foyer, a place for patrons to meet up and wait for groups to form. We also host cocktail parties here some evenings." She led him past small groups of women who politely nodded and exchanged greetings with her. They either ignored him or cast looks that made him want to shrink away. "The first exhibit is behind that door." She pointed to a large carved door that bore only a simple plaque: DENUDED.

Despite the size of the door it opened easily and Elizabeth led him into a brightly lit room. The exhibit was in the center of the room. She tugged on his leash and led him forward. "There can be as many as five million hairs, of various types and in various places, on the human body. I believe that the male body looks better devoid of hair. This is a practical exhibit that attains that goal…in a most elaborate manner."

It took a moment for him to take in exactly what he was seeing. A naked male was fastened to an array of gleaming chrome bars: wrists, ankles, legs, thighs, fore-arms, head, neck, torso, everything seemed to be fastened to a piece of machinery. A tug on his leash brought his eyes down to a console.

"It's easy to operate; a guest simply selects the body position," Elizabeth pointed to a series of 'stick figures' showing the human body in various positions, "and the machine automatically adjusts the subject to that posture. Up here," she jerked his head upwards, "we have a selection of tools." He gazed at the array of gleaming tweezers of every shape and description and magnifying glasses suspended from silver chains. "I've seen guests spend hours here, chatting, and slowly removing the hairs from the subject."

"You mean," he backed away, but she held firm with the leash.

"Yes, it's an interactive exhibit where the male body is plucked clean of all unsightly *male fur*." She laughed, "Perhaps a demonstration?" She punched a but-ton and the machine whirred; within seconds the subject was before her, upside down. "This is a good angle for nose hairs, they're quite sensitive." She reached up and pulled down a set of shiny tweezers. "Nice and s-l-o-w, so they can f-e-e-l it. See," she held up the tweezers, a black hair in the pincers. The man in the machine made an unintelligible moaning sound. She plucked out two more. "Sometimes it makes their eyes water, the nose hairs. How about a few eyelashes?" She plucked out three eyelashes.

Simon tried to pull away, but she held fast to his leash. "You're crazy, you can't do this."

"But I am. This exhibit is very popular. Depending on the crowds, and the hirsute nature of the specimen, we can de-hair a male or two over the course of the exhibit." The subject mumbled again.

"Can't they speak?" Simon asked.

"We considered gagging them, but the staff decided they like that interactive verbal response. Sometimes there may be four or more women working on a subject. It becomes a competition to see who can extract the loudest or most unique response."

Simon felt his knees go weak.

"Of course no one is really interested in *hearing* what a male has to say, so we've injected their vocal chords with a chemical that renders them incapable of intelligible speech. There is the side effect them losing speech capability forever, but we considered that, and don't see that as an impediment."

Simon shook his head in disbelief, "All…all the hairs…all?"

Her hand slid to his collar and she pulled him nose-to-nose, "Every - single - hair. You ought to see them squeal when we go to work on their cock, balls and ass. We can make it last for hours; some of our visitors videotape it."

They watched as three well-dressed women, obviously executives on their lunch hour, sat down and reached above them, pulling down tweezers and magnifying glasses. "Set the machine for balls Linda, let's clean up that scrotum." They shared a laugh as the machine rotated into position, the hapless subject making gurgling noises that Simon could only guess were pleas for mercy. *Not likely, from these bitches!*

"Ready to see more?"

Simon shivered as he left the exhibit, the squeals of the man echoed as the hairs were individually plucked. Even though he was naked he knew the room wasn't cold, but still, he shook. *I can leave whenever I want, overpower these demonic bitches and walk out.* But he allowed himself to be led away, padded along on bare feet behind the high heels of his guide - his benefactor. Was it his curiosity, his reporter's inquisitive nose looking for that break-out story that kept him docile, leashed and naked? Or was it something else? Fight or flight - or the third choice - submit.

"This next one is my favorite, both for the fashion aspect and the clever double-entendre." As with the first, the signage was classically simple: MEN ARE HEELS. Elizabeth opened the door and pulled him into the room.

Paintings of women dominating men adorned the walls, but the eye was immediately drawn to the two pair of GIANT high heels that took up the center of the room. A pair of red shoes and leopard shoes, both in a classic high-heeled pump style dominated the surroundings.

Simon gazed in awe at their imposing size. *They have to be close to seven feet high. OK, big shoes, but what's so special...*

She watched his look change, smiled as the realization swept over him. She allowed his leash the necessary slack so he could approach the towering spike heels. "Lovely aren't they?" she purred. "Simply divine."

He came face to face with the clear acrylic heel,

locking eyes with the face of the male trapped inside. "There's…there's somebody in there."

She laughed; for a writer, an *intellectual*, he seemed a bit slow. "Men are heels, in this case…literally."

His hand rubbed the smooth surface, "They're alive." The heels were clear acrylic, six feet tall, and shaped like a classic spike heel. Inside was a hairless male, facing forward toward the shoe's sole, somehow crammed in so he filled the heel and was completely immobile.

"Of course they're alive; imagine how they'd begin to smell if they were dead. And you can torment the live ones; it is, after all, another interactive exhibit." She picked up a leather whip and lashed out at the back of the heel. A pitiful wail emanated from the shoe. "We left their buttocks exposed. Imagine being punished and you can't get away, escape, movement is impossible. They're trapped with the realization that they must endure whatever anyone wants to administer." She moved to the front of the spike heel, the side facing the sole. "Their nipples were left exposed as well," she viciously grabbed one, violently pinching and twisting it. The heel squealed. "Beautiful, how exquisitely they suffer."

Simon looked to one of the other shoes where a mother and daughter were tormenting a 'heel' delighting in the different cries they were coaxing from it.

A tug on the leash got his attention. "Did you notice their feet?" Elizabeth pointed a perfectly manicured nail to the base of the heel. "Get down on your knees for a closer look."

There was an authority in her voice that made him follow without hesitation, and he dropped to his knees to get a closer look at the heel.

"Ballet heels, eight inches. We put them in ballet heels before we insert them into the heels. The ridiculously high arch gives the foot that delightful stiletto end that makes them so sexy, don't you think?"

Simon couldn't imagine how feet could be put in that position. "Isn't it painful, I mean –"

"Pain? Of course, but male suffering and humiliation are essential parts of my exhibit's theme." With a short leather strap she whipped the heel's exposed cock and balls, her eyes closing and a smile forming as he screamed. She jerked on the leash, "Up!"

Simon felt his balls shrink and his ass clench, he couldn't deny his fear. "Y – you say the exhibit runs for nine weeks. At night…are they…released…"

"No, all males in all exhibits 'assume the position' for the duration of the exhibit. I have a medical staff that comes in at night; they hydrate them, evacuate them with enemas, feed them."

Simon pointed to the hideous shoes on the 'heel's feet'. "But those shoes, I mean wearing them–"

"Yes, it's very likely these particular subjects will be unable to walk afterwards." Her tone held no compassion; rather she discussed the males as commodities. "We're considering options, permanently breaking and reforming all the bones in the foot to the ballet heel shape so they can be permanently used in the shoe exhibit, or selling them off to a unique foreign petting zoo, where wealthy Asian women keep male pets. After all, they can still crawl around like an animal and the throat treatment leaves them able to bark."

Simon looked at the human form molded into the acrylic heel; its eyes seem to say 'run away' but Simon remained frozen in place, tethered to the firm hand of Elizabeth Stansbury, Dominant Patron of the Arts.

"So, what do you think of my exhibit?"

He was incredulous. *Surely she can't get away with this; she's insane, a madwoman.* Yet the exhibit was well attended; women of every age and ethnicity, in groups and singles, roamed the exhibits: looking, touching and tormenting. They greeted Elizabeth and ignored him; *She leads around a naked man, on a leash, and they don't bat an eye.*

She snapped her fingers. "There's one more I'd like you to see; come along, like a good boy." He obediently allowed himself to be led away.

HALL of PAIN read the simple bronze plaque on the final door. "It's important to have a big ending, something memorable, don't you think?" She pulled him close with a tug on the leash. "Are you getting the story you wanted?"

Surely she's not going to just let me walk out of here and write about this? He shivered again.

She saw his fear; she'd noted it all the way through the exhibits. *All that bravado, on the surface, but when faced with reality they crumble, submit, crawl.* "Attendance is better than we projected, if it keeps up we'll open in Atlanta in September. The exit is after this final exhibit."

"OK…yea…great…"

She leaned in, her hot breath on his ear, "Then

let's finish…shall we?" Despite her latent malevolence he couldn't help but be excited by the brush of her hair on his shoulder and the hint of her perfume. She opened the door, "After you."

The Hall of Pain was a popular exhibit. Visitors strolled endlessly up and down, watching large video screens with changing colors. A strange cacophony of sounds: moans, cries and wails filled the air, bringing smiles to the visitor's faces. The volume increased when a group of Goth girls, resplendent in heavy black eye makeup, leather, tattered T-shirts and wicked boots stomped their way up and down the hall. "This is their favorite exhibit," Elizabeth explained.

She led him to a small kiosk. "Good afternoon, Susan."

"Good afternoon, Ms Stansbury." The petite red-head in the kiosk handed Elizabeth a pair of black patent pumps.

"Thank you, Susan, a good crowd today?"

"Oh, yes, very enthusiastic, it's been quite noisy."

"That's what we want." Elizabeth led her naked reporter to a line of benches and sat down. She handed him the black pumps and extended her foot. "Put the shoes on me."

Simon was no longer functioning as a reporter, he was now in a survival mode, his only intent to *get through here and get out!* He knelt and slipped the expensive designer heels from her feet, Prada, he noticed. The new heels were cheaper fetish shoes with five inch metal spike heels. He slipped them on her feet and decided *they look hot, even on an older woman in a fancy suit.*

She stood, now even taller than he, and led him

into the exhibit. The tall spindly heels didn't slow her stride, she moved effortlessly, keeping a pace that had his leash tight. She stopped and spun on one of the wicked heels. "You may notice several women wearing the same shoes. It's part of the exhibit, they get them at the kiosk, loaners from Susan." She chuckled, "Our version of renting bowling shoes…with a diabolical side."

He silently nodded, *let me get this over with and get the hell out of here*. The mother and daughter from the high heel exhibit had now made it to this exhibit and were exchanging their shoes for the wicked metal stilettos.

Elizabeth pointed to them, "Watch."

Simon saw the two women walk from the benches where they changed their shoes and onto the main floor. They shared a smile as they stepped on the main exhibit floor. Their sexy, seductive gait now changed; their steps were deliberate, up and down rather than gliding. They stopped in front of one of the ever-changing colored video screens, but kept their feet in motion: stepping up and down, putting all the weight on one heel and rotating it. As they did they laughed and pointed at the screen, noting the changing designs and colors.

Elizabeth noted Simon's confused look. *Poor baby, it's all been too much for him, but thankfully, or not, we're near the end.* "The floor, darling," she directed his attention to the floor. "Get on your hands and knees and crawl over to get a good look."

He hesitated.

"Go on," she urged, "on your knees." She put her hand on his shoulder and gently pushed him down. "Crawl."

He crawled forward, Elizabeth walking behind

holding his leash, much as she might walk a pet on a Sunday afternoon. The mother and daughter smiled at the scene; Elizabeth nodded at them and returned the smile.

When he got close enough to see the floor details he stopped and backed away in fear. Elizabeth stopped him with a carefully planted metallic spike heel in his exposed bottom. "STAY!"

Panic filled his face, "They're hands...f-fingers." A woman walked by, so close he saw the wicked heels trod over the exposed fingers. He started to rise when he felt the sting of a whip lash his buttocks.

"I SAID STAY DOWN!" Elizabeth flicked the whip again and he howled, but stayed on his knees.

He shook with fear, afraid to remain, afraid to try and leave. *Where did she get a whip?*

"Yes, dear, hands and fingers - male hands and fingers. And yes, they're alive - they feel the pain, the agony, every blissful second of it. It's wonderful isn't it, a patchwork, a mosaic of fingers interlocked to make a human carpet. The males stand below, their hands pro-truding, and the fingers are super-glued to the floor, quite immobilized."

"No, no, no..."

Despair, hopelessness, I love them at this point, so pitiful, so ready to be utilized. "Yes, down below the males are crammed together like cattle, their feet shod in eight-inch ballet boots. Can you imagine, weeks on point while your hands and fingers are continually mauled by women in killer shoes. I mean, really, men have this fascination with women in heels, so why not let them enjoy it...*first hand?*"

"No, please, I...please, no..."

"All the men are gagged and each gag is attached to a tube of a different length. As our subjects moan and wail they do so at different frequencies. These *musical* tones are converted to colors and patterns on the video displays on the walls, real-time performance art."

He thought about the mother and daughter, standing, digging their stilettos into the floor, listening to the sounds and watching the colors. He remembered the Goth girls, stomping up and down the hall.

"That's right; my visitors create their own individual art works, real time, at the expense of the males beneath their high heels." She jerked his leash, "Time to go," and led him across the floor. He followed, watching her stilettos dig into the flesh all the way across the room.

When the wooden door closed behind them, he welcomed the silence. He felt her hands remove the collar.

"I hope you enjoyed the tour; I'm quite looking forward to your article. You'll find your clothes in the dressing room behind that gray door."

He heard her heels click away and turned to see her exit through an elaborately carved wooden door. *Shit! I didn't think she was gonna let me leave. She's certifiable, a fuckin' wack job.* He jumped to his feet and looked around. He was alone. *I'm outta here, and I'm taking this bitch down.* He opened the door and on a chair were his clothes and personal effects. He quickly pulled on his pants and bent over to slip on his shoes…when he felt the prick on the back of his neck. "What the…"

He tried to stand but fell to the floor. Through a haze he saw Caroline; she looked even taller from the floor.

His blonde tormenter held a syringe. "It was a

neuro-muscular agent. You can't move, makes the males easier to handle." He saw her smile and pick up a different syringe. "You didn't really think we were going to let you walk out of here." She bent down; her hand stroked the hair on his arm and chest; she smiled. She held the needle to his neck. "Any intelligible last words?"

"No, no, please – you can't. I won't say-" He felt the needle plunge into his neck. "Please, if you let me gg igh mmgghh, ghgh…"

Elizabeth left her office early to meet her luncheon date. She greeted Debra Parker in the foyer and the women embraced. "Debra, it's so good to see you, you look marvelous."

"Thank you, yes, life is much better with those pesky annoyances removed. I can never thank you enough."

"It was my pleasure, a pleasant afternoon's diversion." Elizabeth took Debra's arm in hers. "Would you like to see him? We're starting him off in the DENUDED exhibit, and we'll move him later, when there's no hair left."

"I can't wait; I've been looking forward to this…for a long time."

"There were four working on him when I last checked."

Simon heard the clicking of more heels as additional visitors entered the room. Some watched, and others stayed to torment and torture a hapless male. The machine whirred and jerked, he was being repositioned. When he came to rest, he was upside down, spread-eagled. It took a moment for him to orient himself and focus; when he did his blood ran cold…Debra.

"Hello, Simon, long time, no see. I never did get that article you were supposed to write." She reached up and pulled down a pair of tweezers. "Are you still doing research? Going undercover?"

He blinked as the tweezers came close to his eyes and he felt that twinge as an eyelash was removed.

"Hold still," she mocked, "we don't want to put out an eye with one of these things." She pulled out a second eyelash.

"Try some of the nose hairs, they often make their eyes water," Elizabeth advised .

Debra adjusted his position and pulled down a magnifying glass and went to work on his right nostril. Within seconds he was moaning. She clapped her hands, "This is fun!"

Elizabeth smiled, "I'm glad I could bring you two back together. I could order in lunch, we could stay here for a while, get re-acquainted."

Debra held up a long hair she'd plucked from Simon's nose. "Lunch would be wonderful, thank you. I don't have to be back at work until two."

"It will be our little afternoon reunion then," Elizabeth smiled, "just the three of us."

END

"You have been sentenced to life imprisonment for crimes against GenEngineering Labs and against women. We couldn't let you simply walk away, given what you knew about our research.

"You're small, approximately eleven and a half inches tall; now a member of our Organic Miniaturization Project. You'll be glad to know that you're still part of GenEngineering Labs, a small part." She laughed at her pun.

"Although you won't be drawing a check, we will give you," she laughed, "room and board."

Mini Men Lesbian Village

Karen's eyes opened as the red, blinking lights illuminated the room. *Shit! Five minutes, I've got five minutes to make it to the feeding trough.* It had only taken two instances of being late to know the punishments were severe for non-performance. She looked across the room; Dee Dee was already up. They both slipped on their shoes and ran down the hall.

TWO MONTHS Earlier.....

"Bastards!" Elena Nováková ripped at the duct tape and removed the doll crudely taped to her office door. Inside, she kicked the door shut and dropped her briefcase to the floor. *Assholes, why do they do this?*

She carefully placed the doll on her desk, as one might a real child, and gently straightened the arms and legs. Slowly she removed the duct tape, as if to do it too quickly would harm the lifeless plastic form. She used an alcohol wipe to remove the sticky tape residue, her last act softly brushing out the doll's golden hair.

Someone, *probably Karl*, used a black permanent marker to draw pubic hairs on the doll. Elena reverently put the doll in her desk drawer, *Tonight I'll take you home and clean you up, it's OK now.*

She rose and removed her suit coat, exchanging it for the white lab coat emblazoned with 'Dr. Nováková, Director, GenEngineering Labs', *Director, it's a long way from a poor Czech farm with no electricity.* Her eyes caught a reflection in the glass of one of her many diplomas: PhDs in Electrical Engineering, Genetics and Molecular Biology. The face looking back at her retained its youthful appearance: deep brown eyes on a round face, not fat, but filled out enough to smooth away the wrinkles that might mar the complexion of any other thirty-five year old career woman. Her hair, yes, it always needed something. *Hairstyle on farm is a matter of function, not fashion.* She ran her fingers through the shaggy brown tresses that fell to her shoulders and made a mental note to see Jenny, who would do something about her hair.

Static and the voice from her intercom nudged her back to business, "Dr. Nováková, they're ready for you now."

Elena saw the smirks on Karl and Dwight's faces as she entered the conference room. For a moment she held their gaze, dropped the sheaf of papers on the polished mahogany surface and took her seat at the head of the table.

A junior researcher poured coffee for everyone while another booted up the computer. Charts and graphics filled the high resolution screen at the far end of the room. Elena nodded her thanks for the coffee and pulled her glasses from her coat pocket. She brushed the ever-present hair from her eyes and slipped on her glasses. The room was silent while she studied the first page of the report. "Steven, give us your report on the Beta test group."

A tall thin man, his graying hair pulled into a pony tail, stepped to the screen. "Can we have the first slide?" He took a laser pointer from the rostrum and directed the red beam to the screen.

It was going to be a long meeting, and underneath the conference table Elena quietly worked her feet out of the designer pumps she wore to such occasions. It was never easy, balancing being a research scientist, corporate executive, and a woman. The high heels were a concession to the image of being the senior female executive of GenEngineering Labs. And she noted the different way the men, scientist and non-scientist alike, treated her when she wore them.

Steven Keller continued his briefing. "We had mixed results from the first strains, depending on the various radiation protocols used." His pointer illuminated on several columns of figures. "The raw data is in the secure distributed data base, available for download," he noted. "There were indications of the molecular changes we're seeking, but we're still analyzing all the variables to make sure it's not a random occurrence, although we did maintain a rigid control group. Next slide, please."

The slide dissolved and half of another slide appeared on the screen. It too was filled with columns of numbers and formulae. Steven paused and smiled, milking his moment. "And then we tried the developmental serum, again, along with the radiation protocol, but we timed the radiation protocol, administering it at the same time the serum began to metabolize within the cellular structure. And…" He nodded to the research assistant at the computer and the rest of the slide came up. It was a video, showing several rats in a cage, half of them full size and the others less than one-quarter of the size of the larger ones.

Karl laughed, more of a snort than a laugh, and made a show of dropping his pencil on the table. "And your specimens had babies!" he guffawed. He snapped his finger and held out his coffee cup to the research assistant in the corner of the room.

Elena shot Karl an angry glance and he looked away from her. She hurriedly slipped her feet back into her heels, rose and walked to the screen. The room was silent as everyone watched her remove her glasses, and closely study the animals scurrying around in their cage.

"Yea, baby rats," Dwight chirped.

"Quiet!" Elena snapped. She didn't have to turn around to know that he'd shut up, that everyone was looking at he and Karl, and that both of them were seething at being reprimanded - by her.

She continued to intently study the animals, pausing to look up and smile at Steven. Her fingers traced one of the smaller rats on the screen as it ran around the cage. "These," her eyes locked on Steven's, "these are not baby rats."

Steven's own eyes twinkled. "No, they are not baby rats. And they were," he paused, savoring this long awaited moment. "They were…full sized."

Her hands clutched his white lab coat. "You did it!" It should have been a shout, but it was barely a whisper. The assembled throng at the table leaned forward to catch some of the conversation from the front of the room.

Elena spun on her heel, her eyes quickly finding the only non-lab-coated figure in the room. Parker Westgate sat in the corner of the room in his usual dark blue suit, white shirt and regimental striped tie. His close cropped graying hair, cold gray eyes, and military bearing clearly set him apart from the roomful of scientists. A hardened ex-SAS commando, he was GenEngineering Labs Head of Security. Whether or not he'd really assassinated a foreign diplomat, it made for great gossip, and allowed him a wide berth from the scientific community.

"I want total security lockdown - now!" Elena ordered.

Parker stood, curtly nodded, took his cell phone from his belt and whispered orders into the phone.

Elena surveyed the room. "No one leaves the room without signing a new non-disclosure statement."

Excitement buzzed around the table: "Did Steven do it?" "Did they make the breakthrough?" "It must be the serum and radiation combination." "Shit, the stock is gonna go through the roof."

"Quiet!" Elena turned, making eye contact with each person. "Research is a slow and deliberative process; we make haste slowly. Steven's group has made significant progress in the Organic Miniaturization Project, but there is much work to do. We must replicate, document and test. We must maintain control - and security." She turned to Parker, "No leaks."

Parker opened the door and admitted two members of his security team, who walked to the table, opened their briefcases and handed out new non-disclosure agreements to everyone in the room.

Steven followed Elena to her office, where they both sat on the leather couch.

Elena's domineering executive manner was now replaced with the giddy enthusiasm of discovery. "You did it!"

Steven shrugged and nodded, his grin becoming a smile. "My team did it. Your team, Elena; you're the boss here."

"I want to examine the specimens," she said. "Are they normal, no noted abnormalities?"

"We need to do more tests, do post mortems on some and examine the cellular structure, study some of the others for longer-term effects, but so far" Steven spread his hands, "they behave like normal lab rats."

Elena gazed out the window, watching dark clouds creep across the horizon; it would rain by this afternoon. "Amazing, we've managed to reduce the size a living organic system, in essence, to shrink it. The systemic ramifications are – unbelievable."

"There is still much to do," Steven offered.

"Yes, yes," Elena waved her hand, "You're right;

I know. But still, it *is* a breakthrough."

"My team has prepared a full briefing for you, tomorrow, at ten. We think you'll be pleased."

Elena spent the rest of the day going over Steven's data, eagerly anticipating the full briefing and examination the next day. When she reached into her desk she saw the doll, and thought of Karl and Dwight. They mocked her fascination with dolls. *Assholes!* It was no secret that collecting dolls was her primary non-scientific passion. Some of the behaviorists on the clinical staff theorized that it was her poor Eastern-bloc upbringing that made her compensate by collecting things she never had as a child. Regardless of the motivation, her house was filled with shelves of dolls, and she routinely prowled the weekend Flea Markets and Garage Sales in search of hidden doll treasures, clothes and furniture. Her basement contained an elaborate doll house where she housed her prize collections in surreal, miniature settings. Bookshelves were full of doll catalogues and doll collecting reference books.

When it was time to leave for the day she locked the files in her office safe, and for extra security, changed the biometric fingerprint key to a different finger than she'd used before. She made a mental note to change it daily. Her final act was to wrap the doll in a silk scarf and carefully place in her briefcase.

The rain pelted her expensive SUV as she pulled from the executive parking garage. The weather made the traffic worse and she cursed the fact that she'd be late getting home. She stopped for takeout chicken; *too late to cook.*

The street lights had come on, casting both shadows and glistening shafts of light from the pools of rain in the street. Elena pulled into the driveway and flicked on the garage door opener. *Big American house, expensive European car, so different from...*

Elena never forgot her roots, her humble beginnings. Her father had died on that farm, toiled all his life and died - working there. When she graduated from college and started earning the money of a PhD Elena moved her mother to a nice apartment in Karlovy Vary. As a visiting lecturer at many European Universities she visited her mother several times a year, enjoying the waters of the famous spa town.

She carried her chicken and briefcase to the dining room table and quickly set a place for herself with a china plate and silverware. She took a bottle of wine from the refrigerator and stopped to grab a book from the bookshelf. Before she ate, she took the doll from her briefcase. Her attention was on the doll, and as she thumbed through the book, she read aloud, only casually taking bites of chicken and cole slaw. "Ah, here you are. You are 1985 Sally Anne doll. It says you were made between 1983 and 1987, and that you were Ginger's best friend. I have a Ginger. We'll get you some clothes later."

Later that evening Elena descended the stairs to her basement doll world, the indulgence of a successful scientist/executive who'd made a place for herself in the world – all the way from a poor Czech farm. She walked directly to a cabinet and opened the drawer that she knew contained the perfect outfit for Sally Anne. Much as a loving mother would, Elena carefully dressed the doll, choosing just the right plastic shoes and purse, from an accessories drawer. She held the doll at arm's length, smiled and placed it on the shelf next to Sally's best friend Ginger.

Elena walked to the far end of the room, where her custom-made dollhouse took up much of the wall. She busied herself arranging the various dolls: the mother in her shirtwaist dress standing at the stove, the teen doll wearing her first high heels in her bedroom, another doll posing in front of a cheval mirror. When she wasn't authoring scientific journal articles or leading ground-breaking research Elena enjoyed her dolls. She smiled as she ascended the stairs and turned out the light.

Elena stepped from the shower and grabbed a towel, wrapping it around her. Her feet left damp foot prints as she tracked across her bedroom to the phone. It hadn't stopped ringing since she'd entered the shower. In an hour she'd be at work, who could be calling her now? The phone nearly slipped from her wet hand, "Yes?"

"Elena, it's –"

"Yes, Parker, what is it?" She immediately recognized his clipped British tones.

"There's been a leak." His voice was even, but Elena heard the underlying urgency. "It's on the web. Spencer is on his way in."

Spencer Bachman was the GenEngineering Labs Public Affairs Officer. Elena glanced at her bedside clock,

"Eight-thirty, my office." She and Parker hung up simultaneously. "Hovno!"

When Elena reached her office she found Parker and Spencer waiting with Gretchen, her secretary. Joining them was Mark Fuller, Parker's Deputy Information Security Officer. Elena's secretary followed them into her office and brought coffee. "Thank you," Elena said, "hold my calls, no one comes in."

Gretchen nodded and backed out, shutting the door behind her.

Elena ripped open a package of diet sweetener and stirred it into her coffee. "One day! Not even a full day! What happens in one day?"

Parker handed her a file folder. "It's on the Internet, 'GenEngineering Labs Makes Breakthrough in Micro-Biology Molecular Engineering.' There's no real specifics, but it clearly references the progress of Steven's group."

Between sips of her coffee Elena read the screen printouts. "Do you have a source?"

"No," Parker answered, "Mark's working on it."

Elena looked at Parker and Spencer, "Options?"

"Don't deny, instead deflect it, spin it," Spencer offered. "I can issue a release 'Yes the Organic Miniaturization Project is one of the many on-going research efforts at GenEngineering Labs. We've made small progress and are continuing, but are still years away from clinical trials and ultimate FDA approval of any applications.' In a couple of days some teen singer will be arrested for drunk driving and we'll be old news. It's best not to over react, or deny."

Elena laughed; *Americans live in the moment*, and turned to look at Parker.

"I agree," Parker said. His eyes locked on Elena's, "There is…more."

Elena held his gaze and then turned to Spencer. "Write up a release, but bring it to me, I need to run it by the board before we go public. We must move on this, put it down – today – this morning."

Spencer stood, "I'm on it," and left the room.

Elena paused to look at Parker and Mark. "What is it?"

Parker nodded to Mark who handed Elena yet another file folder. "There was a large stock buy, two of them in fact, for shares of GenEngineering stock."

Elena studied the data, hundreds of thousands of dollars in stock purchases. She looked at Parker and Mark. "A leak on the internet and two stock purchases… So close in time, coincidence?" She studied Parker's cold eyes as he shook his head 'no' and imagined those same eyes peering down a sniper's scope. Her Uncle had been a sniper for the partisans during the war.

Mark continued, "I was able to identify the stock purchasers."

Elena didn't ask 'how' he'd done that; she was content to have the information. "And…"

Parker reached into his pocket and removed two photographs, the typical GenEngineering Labs pictures that were on every employee security badge. He slid them face down across the desk.

Elena's fingers pulled the photographs to her and she slowly turned them over. *Karl! Dwight!* Rage flashed in her brown eyes and her jaw tightened. "Detain them!"

Dwight Coglin paced the room, stopping to whisper at Karl, "She fucking knows! Somehow they found out."

Karl slammed his diet cola on the table. "Get a grip; they've got nothing. I covered our tracks. Keep your cool and it'll be OK. They're just fishing, looking for anything." He looked again at the closed door, knowing that outside lurked one of Parker's ex-Marine security goons. Clearly there were no overweight and aging rent-a-cops working security here. GenEngineering Labs security could topple a small third-world country.

Dwight ran his hands through his hair, sat down and rose again to pace the room once more. "No, no - she knows. Shit, we're finished."

Karl Wainright loosened his tie and threw the empty can into the corner wastebasket. "Our doll-playing Lesbian bitch doesn't know shit; told you, she's fishing, trying to sweat us."

"Yea, right, your thing with the doll only pissed her off more." Dwight was the weaker of the two, the follower, and now regretted his alliance with Karl. "And how do you know she's a Lesbian? 'Cause she wouldn't sleep with you?"

An uneasy silence settled over the room. They waited.

Elena handed the press release to Spencer. "Excellent work, the board and I approve. Release it...and make yourself available to any media outlets, full and open disclosure, only don't tell them anything." Elena trusted Spencer. They'd hired him from the Washington Beltway where he'd been a press spokesman for any number of agencies and individuals. He could talk for days without saying anything, driving away bored reporters who left in search of 'real' stories.

"No problem, we'll stay on top of it, anything changes, you'll be the first to know." Spencer left Elena and Parker alone in the office.

Elena turned to Parker and arched her eyebrows.

"I think we have a handle on it," Parker said, "at least the internet leak. And after all, the whole shrinking thing *is* a bit fantastic." He raised a conciliatory hand when he saw her eyes narrow. "I'll admit, I don't understand the science, but I also don't doubt the talent you've put together on this project, the money that's been invested in it, or the strides you've made. I think that on the face of it, the entire incident will soon blow over. But…we still have a problem."

Elena sat back in her chair and closed her eyes, "Karl and Dwight, the source of the leaks and our stock manipulators. Yes…" She came back to an upright position and looked at Parker. "Our options? Terminate them and make them sign a non-disclosure agreement as part of their severance?"

Parker's face was impassive. "We saw how well they honored yesterday's non-disclosure agreement."

Elena's shoulders slumped, her head dropped to her chest.

"Do you want me to make the problem…go away?" Parker asked.

She slowly raised her head to look at him. His expression hadn't changed. *Make the problem go away.* As a girl she'd heard the stories of black cars in the night, people disappearing, State problems 'going away.'

"They can't be trusted, can't be put back on the project, can't be terminated without risking that they'll sell everything they know to a competitor." Parker took a sip from a bottle of water. "What do you want me to do?"

Elena's eyes scanned the room, searching for an answer; she was angry, but not enough to take their lives. *There is always a solution, think outside the box.* She saw Steven's briefing book on his research project. She leaned across her desk and Parker leaned in closer as well. "Here is what I want you to do," she whispered.

Karl and Dwight jumped as the doorknob turned and the two security men entered the room. "Sorry for any inconvenience doctors," said the taller of the two, "you're free to go."

"Yea, right," grumbled Karl. "Somebody's gonna hear about this."

Dwight struggled to get his arm back into his jacket and hoped Karl would shut up. He wanted out without any additional problems.

The second security man held the door open, "You're both to go back to work."

Karl continued to rage against the company, Parker and Elena, and failed to notice the security man move behind him. He was questioning Parker's parentage when he felt the pinprick on his neck. "What the fu-" Before he could fall to the floor the security man caught him and slumped him in a chair.

Dwight looked up in horror and bolted for the door, but the second security man caught him in a wrist lock and Dwight too felt the pinprick.

The security man removed the radio from his belt and called Parker Westgate. "It's done."

He awoke in total darkness. He'd never known such blackness; he literally couldn't see his hand in front of his face. He sat up, tried to stand, but felt lightheaded and fell back to his hands and knees. He sat. His hands felt the surface below him, polished smooth. Glass? Marble? *Damn, it's dark. Where...* His hand brushed his leg; he was naked. In the darkness his hands explored his body. Not only was he naked, he was hairless. Karl had always been rather hirsute, but now his body was not only hairless, but smooth...and soft. "Hello? Hello? Is anybody there? Where am I?"

Elena watched the greenish figure in her night vision goggles. Darkness and silence were formidable weapons for breaking someone's will. She watched as the figure continued to call out, only his shrill voice breaking the quiet in the room.

He placed his hands before him and slowly walked through the darkness, to the edge of his confinement. When his hands found the same hard, smooth surface as the floor he stopped, running them up and down, left and right. He felt no edge, no change, and cautiously followed the wall.

She watched as he carefully moved to the right, exploring the bounds of his prison.

"Hello, is anyone there? Where am I?" He continued to walk, never finding the edge of the room, the corner. *I'm going around in circles.* He stopped and dropped to his knees and felt the floor again, but everything was the same cold, hard, smooth surface.

When he jumped up Elena tried not to laugh. In his nakedness his cock and balls bobbed shamelessly. He jumped again and again, reaching higher, searching for the ceiling, for escape, for… Finally he stopped, dropped to his knees and beat his fists on the floor.

Elena stifled a chuckle; she didn't want to give away the fact she was in the room, watching his plunge into despair. *Jumping to touch the ceiling; how absurd! He'll never reach it, after all, it's well over twenty-four inches high!*

She returned two hours later and found his green-hued form slumped against the edge of his prison. She set down the tray she was carrying, watching him react to the noise she deliberately made.

His head jerked up and he looked around, still unable to see in the black void. "Who's there? Someone please help me."

Elena spoke into a microphone, a special sound editing program giving her voice an unearthly, detached quality. "Crawl forward two times and kneel up with your hands behind your head."

"Please, you have to help me. Can you turn on a light?"

"Crawl forward two times and kneel up with your hands behind your head."

"Fuck you! Somebody help me!" he screamed.

"Disobedience is punished." Elena picked up the pitcher of ice water and walked to the Plexiglas cylinder. She slowly poured the icy water into the top, watching as it filtered through the many holes in the top and emerged as an icy deluge on the figure below. She heard him gasp from the bone chilling cold.

He wrapped his arms around himself and ran wildly bumping into the sides of his small prison. There was no refuge from the frigid onslaught. The water rose to his knees, slowing his progress. "What do you want!?!" he screamed.

"Kneel up with your hands behind your head."

The water was moving up his thighs. "Please, please, stop!"

Elena stopped pouring water and engaged the small, hidden drain. When the cylinder was empty she left him once again, still alone, naked and in the dark, but now wet and cold.

For the next two hours he shivered, screamed and cried. Out of nowhere came the ethereal voice. "Crawl forward two times and kneel up with your hands behind your head."

Even as begged, "Please, please," he crawled forward and assumed the position.

"What is your name?"

"My name is Karl Wainright and I'm a scientist-"

Elena measured a half-cup of ice water and poured

it over him. "Your name is Karen."

He screamed from the cold and shook his fists. "WHO ARE YOU?"

"What is your name?"

"I told you, my name is-" The water hit him again.

"Your name is Karen. What is your name?"

His body racked with sobs as he choked out, "K-Karen. Where-where am I?"

The water drenched him again, followed by the voice. "You do not ask questions."

His body shook with chills and his breath came in short gasps.

"Do you know why you are here?"

His head shook, his voice weaker now, "N-n-no."

"You are guilty of treason, theft, insolence to women, and failure to honor your profession. Your sentence - life imprisonment."

He felt a blanket fall from above and curled up in a fetal form, clutching the blanket to his shivering body. The voice was gone, all was silence and blackness.

Elena was in another room, once more watching the green figure in the darkness. This one knelt in a proper form, its posture perfect. "What is your name?"

The response was immediate, "Dee Dee."

Elena smiled; Dwight had been much easier, as she knew he would be.

The light was blinding and Karl threw up his hands as he screamed. He peeked through slits in his fingers and turned three-sixty. The glaring lights came from every direction; he saw nothing beyond them. Just as quickly they went off, and then slowly the room filled with light. Karl was finally able to verify his current habitat; it was indeed some sort of Plexiglas cylinder. He was enclosed, naked, on display. A second light switched on across the room and Karl looked to see…Elena Nováková: PhD, executive, and esteemed scientist. But she was…HUGE. She loomed in the chair across the room. In fact, everything in the room was enormous.

His eyes caught the sight of a similar cylinder containing…Dwight! He was naked, kneeling in the center of the cylinder, his hands behind his head, the fingers interlaced. Karl ran to the enclosure wall and banged his fists, "Dwight! Dwight!"

The enclosure was rocked with a sound like the crash of thunder. Karl turned to see Elena sitting in her chair, her outstretched arm holding a wooden cane as she rapped on his closure. "He will not answer you. He knows to do so will bring punishment. Assume the position yourself."

Her other hand raised a crystal pitcher and Karl saw the beads of condensation dripping down the sides. *Ice water*. He dropped to his knees and put his hands behind his head.

Elena's cane struck his enclosure, "What is your name?" She held forth the pitcher.

"Karen."

Elena tapped on Dwight's cage, "What is your name?"

"Dee Dee."

Elena rose and walked across the room, stopping between the clear Plexiglas cages. "Karen and Dee Dee, those are now your names. As I explained to both of you, for your crimes you have been sentenced to life imprisonment, crimes against GenEngineering Labs and against women. We couldn't just let you walk away, given what you knew about our research. You'll be glad to know that you're still part of GenEngineering Labs, a small part." She laughed at her pun. "Although you won't be drawing a check, we will give you," she laughed, "room and board."

She removed a vial and an eye dropper from her pocket, and filled the eye dropper with a green colored viscous liquid. Her hand, which loomed large above her kneeling charges, descended and deposited pools of the gruel in front of each kneeling form. "You are hungry, starvation was part of your conditioning. Eat, it's formulated to meet your essential nutritional needs, though the taste; that wasn't a concern."

Karl and Dwight *were* hungry; they didn't know when they'd eaten last, although they'd had the opportunity to lap up water that pooled in their enclosures. Both men brought their faces to the floor and tentatively lapped at the green goo. Karl made a face and backed away.

Elena struck his enclosure with her cane. "You will eat; it will sustain you. Eat, or it's another session in the dark, in the freezing water. While you eat I'll explain your…situation."

She walked across the room and returned to her seat. "You're small, approximately eleven and a half inches tall. You're part of the test group for our Organic

Miniaturization Project, albeit a very secret and classified part. You'll be studied for long-term effects. Having actual human test subjects might put us years ahead of schedule. By the way, the big stock purchases you made, they funded your current condition and closed a lot of mouths about what happened to you. The last anyone knows, you went underground, some say to Eastern Europe, to sell GenEngineering Labs research data."

Both their heads rose from the floor, their tongues and lips covered in the green, slimy gruel. She saw the surprise and horror in their faces. "Yes, that's right, you're gone, disappeared, non-persons. I doubt anyone is spending much time looking for you."

She walked back to her two specimens and dropped a blanket in each enclosure and then fastened the lids shut. "You two will live here, with me. Tomorrow we'll get you settled in. I'm going to enjoy that." She draped the black shrouds over their cages, plunging them into darkness.

Karl and Dwight awoke when their world literally moved. They tumbled to the side of their enclosures and braced themselves against the smooth walls, remaining on their hands and knees.

She's taking us somewhere, we're being moved. Karl rubbed the sleep from his eyes. Part of him still refused to believe what was happening, she couldn't have done this, it must all be a bad dream, yet his reality never changed.

His environment changed; suddenly his enclosure tilted to its side and he found himself tumbling out, landing beside Dwight in a tangle of naked arms and legs. Wherever they were, it was dark.

"Dwight?"

"Karl?"

They reached out in the darkness, finding and touching each other.

HER voice came out of the darkness. If this was all a dream, it was a nightmare, and they hadn't awoken from it yet. "This is your new home. I'll turn on the lights and let you explore your surroundings. When I return, we'll discuss my rules - and your futures."

They heard footsteps recede and then the lights came on.

They were in a house, in a bedroom, or at least part of a house. One entire wall was glass. They walked to the glass wall, it extended from floor to ceiling. Beyond the wall was a larger room, with shelves full of dolls, book cases, and cabinets. Everything in the room beyond the glass was large, to them.

They pushed and pounded on the glass wall, testing its strength.

Dwight turned, his back against the glass wall, and slumped to the floor. "It's no use; we can't get out that way, we got no tools - no hope."

Karl looked down at his naked companion. "Fuck that shit! Pull yourself together. We can't let this bitch do this to us." He looked around, "C'mon, let's check this out." Karl struggled to think rationally in what appeared to be a totally irrational environment. "We need to assess our environment, identify our strengths and weaknesses."

"Strengths?" Dwight let out a forlorn chuckle and buried his face in his hands. "Strengths? Karl, we're fucking eleven inches tall. She could crush us with one hand."

"So what, you just want to give in? Get up; let's see where we are."

Dwight rose and the two of them moved away from the wall and into the bedroom. It was a normal sized room, for them, everything scaled perfectly to fit a person eleven inches tall. The room contained one king-sized bed, a large dresser, two large armoires, a full length mirror, two slipper chairs and a dressing table with mirror.

"There's nothing but dresses in here," said Dwight. He stood before an open armoire and pulled out a long, purple sequined gown. "It's full of dresses, hats and shoes."

Karl opened the armoire next to him, "Same here." He moved to the dresser and opened a drawer. "This is full of women's clothes too: shorts, shirts." He held up a long purple glove, dropped it back in the drawer and closed it. He turned to see Dwight holding a long pink gown in front of him.

Dwight looked up, "You don't think she means these clothes are for us - do you?"

Karl nodded to the bedroom door, or the space where a door should have been; it was an open doorway. "Let's check this out."

The open doorway led to a spacious bathroom. There was a large bathtub that had what appeared to be a functional faucet and drain for water, but there was no way to control it from the bathroom. Karl smiled; *I bet she's got that figured out*. The shower was enclosed in

Plexiglas. *No privacy, nowhere to hide, always on display.* Karl looked around the room. Each of the rooms they'd been in had been illuminated, but... *No light switches, she controls that too.* They moved through the next open doorway.

The next room was larger, yet sparse in its furnishings, again with a full-length glass wall. Whereas the bedroom was carpeted, this room had a polished wooden floor. Karl knelt to examine it, "Looks like real wood."

"Yea," Dwight said, his tone bitter, "everything *seems* real, but us."

Both men walked around the room; one wall was decorated with workout posters, showing women executing different exercises. Another wall was made up entirely of mirrors. At the far end of the room was a stage with a shiny metal pole extending from the stage to the ceiling.

Karl jumped on the stage and grabbed the pole, pulling on it with all his strength. "Maybe we can use this to break that glass wall. Here, gimme a hand."

Dwight joined him and together they pulled and pushed on the pole.

Elena sipped her tea, her eyes enjoying her naked prisoners struggling with the pole. She laughed at the way their now-miniature cocks and balls bounced as they flailed against the pole. Her finger tapped a key on her keyboard and the 'microphone' icon blinked. "Nice try, my babies, but seriously, you don't think it's going to be *that* easy-do you?"

They both stopped at the sound of the ethereal voice. Their eyes darted to the glass wall, but they were alone in the room.

Dwight pushed away from the pole, his shoulders sagging in obvious despair. "She's watching us. She's ahead of us on every move. We're prisoners."

"Shit!" Karl slapped the pole and then kicked it, stubbing his toe. "SHIT!" He looked at Dwight, *he's defeated, she's broken him.* He grabbed Dwight and pulled him up. "Listen, it's just the two of us and her; you and me, we have to stay together, be strong. OK?"

Dwight nodded his silent agreement.

Karl pointed to the next doorway. "C'mon, we need to survey our environment so we know what we're dealing with, so we can plan."

Plan? thought Dwight. *The only one here with a plan is Elena; we're simply her puppets. And she saw us messing with that pole. Cameras? Video monitoring?*

The next open doorway beckoned, and they moved forward.

A stairwell led them downstairs. The rooms had all been finished with paint or wallpaper and the stairwell was no different. It was covered in a floral, lilac pattern. Framed portraits adorned the walls of the stairwell, pictures of women partially clothed and engaged in sexual activities. Karl found them erotic.

The stairwell emptied into a large living room. The walls were a mixture of deep reds and burgundies, with heavy velvet drapes and overstuffed floral-patterned furniture.

Karl snorted, "Looks like a French whorehouse."

"Yea," said Dwight, "and who do you think the whores are?"

Karl spun on his heel and glared at Dwight.

"She said this is where we were going to live." Dwight pointed to their naked bodies. "Who do you think those clothes upstairs are for?"

Karl ran to the same glass wall that dominated every room. He looked out at the shelves of dolls, all prettily clothed and displayed on their doll stands. "No," he shook his head, "no."

"No? You're the great planner and schemer," Dwight sneered. "What do *you* think this is all about?"

Enraged, Karl ran to grab a lamp off one of the elegant living room tables. It wouldn't budge. He tried to push a chair, but it was immobile. "Shit! Fucking bitch."

"And I thought you were the smart one, Karen. It looks like Dee Dee has it all figured out." Elena's voice once again filled their world and they stopped in their tracks. "Finish your explorations and then we'll have our little talk."

Dwight made his way into the next room, Karl following silently behind. It was the dining room; smooth, polished wood floors, rugs, and elegant dining table and chairs.

Karl tried to move a chair, but it was secured to the floor. "Damn, she's got everything fastened down."

"Yea, not likely we're gonna be able to use anything to break out of here." Dwight looked up at the chandelier that lit the room, even standing on the table it was out of reach.

The last room was the kitchen. It contained all the usual kitchen appliances and furnishings, although all were non-functional mockups, strictly for decoration. A glass trough ran next to the sink.

"What now?" asked Dwight.

Karl shrugged his shoulders. "Go back to the living room and wait for our demonic hostess, I guess."

They waited, the real, full-sized world looming on the opposite side of their impenetrable glass wall. So close, and yet…

The lights went out, they plunged into darkness. Both men waited silently. Suddenly the lights returned, now brighter than ever. They closed their eyes against the glare.

"I control your world, the light and the dark." It was Elena's voice.

The lights dimmed to normal but the men felt a movement in the room: air. The room quickly chilled and the men shivered in the cold. Just as suddenly the air turned warm, then hot.

"I control the hot and the cold." It was her voice, but they could see she was not in the room.

They heard the sound of a door and foot falls on the stairs. Soon Elena loomed into their view and took a seat in front of the glass.

She spread her arms. "So…you like your new home?"

"How long do you intend to keep us here? What about us getting back to normal, can you do that?" Karl asked.

"That's NOT what I asked you," Elena snapped. "Normally you'd be disciplined for insubordination, but since this is all new to you…" She leaned back in her chair. "I'll take your questions in reverse order. Returning to normal? Not possible, even if I wanted to, which I don't. It's not a technology we're pursuing. How long will you be here? Forever, I told you before, you both disappeared, you're fugitives. If people *are* looking for you," she laughed, "it won't be in my basement doll house."

She waited, watching their barely contained fury and frustration. "Any more questions? No? Then let me explain my rules - and your existence. Your names are Karen and Dee Dee. You will answer to those names and address each other by those names only. The clothes you found in the bedroom, the *doll* clothes? Those are your clothes. You will dress every day in the lovely dresses, hats, gloves and shoes that I've prepared for you. You will follow the schedule that is prepared for you each day."

She held up what looked like a hi-tech cell phone and entered a code. Across the room an LCD screen flashed the message. KAREN-BATHE, DEE DEE-SHOWER. "That screen will give you your daily schedule. The water will automatically start and empty." She entered another code: DEE DEE-STRIPPER POLE-45 MINUTES. "Whatever activity you see on the screen you must do." Her eyes narrowed and an evil smile played across her lips as she entered the next code: 69.

Her smile broadened at their quizzical looks. "You're my dolls now, my playthings. And since you're living together in this doll house and wearing dresses - you're Lesbian dolls." She laughed to see their reaction. "Sixty-nine means you two go down on each other. I could have had those things removed," she pointed the the area between their legs, "but I think this will be so much more entertaining."

Karl rose from the sofa and stormed to the glass wall. "You're crazy! Fuckin' certifiable - BITCH!"

She'd expected this, they were so predictable. She

reached down and picked up a Plexiglas cage. When she held it up to their glass wall they both shrank back in terror.

"Gromphadorhina portentosa, also known as the giant Madagascar hissing cockroach. These are almost three inches long. Imagine your lovely doll house infested with them at night. You won't be able to see them, but you'll hear their hissing sound as they make their way to you. Remember, there are no doors."

Karen and Dee Dee backed away from the glass wall as Elena held the cage up so they could see the size of the insects scampering about.

"They eat mostly vegetation, supposedly they're quite docile and make good pets. Then again, with your small size, I'm not sure what they'd do with you." Elena jiggled the cage and the cockroaches hissed. "So, why don't you two kiss each other, right now, or you may have visitors tonight." Elena smiled at their dilemma. Karen and Dee Dee seemed paralyzed with fear: of cockroaches? Of the impending homosexual act? "Do it."

Dee Dee turned to face Karen. "Karl, I can't-"

"KAREN!" barked Elena, "her name is Karen."

"K-Karen, I can't face those bugs." Dee Dee grabbed Karen's head and pulled her into a kiss.

Elena leaned close to the glass, watching as Karen made only a feeble attempt to fight off the kiss. "Yes, you two might as well learn to enjoy it. I expect to see my Lesbian dolls perform quite often. And look at the bright side; it's not as if I'm denying you sexual gratification. In fact, you'll have lots of sex."

She leaned back in her chair and returned the cockroach cage to the floor. "Ok girls, that's enough, go to your bedroom, time to get dressed." Elena laughed as they broke the kiss and wiped their mouths with the back of their hands. *They'll get over that, soon it will be completely natural for them to kiss, hold hands...*

They stood in the bedroom, each holding a long gown in front of them, awaiting Elena's approval.

"Karen, you wear the peach and lavender one. Dee Dee, I want you in the pink gown. You must help each other dress, all the clothes fasten at the back." She laughed as her dolls wiggled into the calf-length gowns. Nearly all the doll clothes were fancy formal gowns. *I like my dolls pretty.* "Turn around, let me see you."

They turned, their leg movements now severely restricted by the long, tight gowns. They were effectively hobbled.

"Very nice," mewed Elena. "Now shoes; pick out shoes to match your dress."

Both dolls rummaged in the armoire for shoes. When they turned back to Elena they were each holding a pair of shoes that matched the color of their dress.

"Excellent, put them on." She laughed as they struggled to cram their feet into the unforgiving plastic shoes. In a year their feet would be ruined. "Walk to the glass so I can get a good look at you."

Karen stumbled and caught herself on the bed.

"My dolls need to learn to walk in long, skin-tight dresses and high heels; that will be the bulk of your wardrobe. Finish your outfits, hats and gloves."

Karen and Dee Dee minced to the dresser to find a pair of long gloves and pull them up their arms.

"There's no fingers, they're like mittens," Karen exclaimed.

"They are gloves for dolls, so you will wear them," Elena ordered, "now hats."

When her dolls were suitably gowned, gloved, high-heeled and hatted Elena ordered them to the exercise room. She punched a code into her cell and the screen flashed: SEXY WALK – ONE HOUR. "This is a sample of your existence; while you practice your walk I will explain other aspects of your daily routine. Your sexy walk is hands on hips, one foot in front of the other, like fashion models. Begin.

"The glass trough in the kitchen is your feeding trough. Twice a day you receive a feeding. It provides all daily nutritional and caloric requirements although it is a gruel and not particularly tasty. It will keep you alive and healthy. If you do not feed - you will be punished.

"The screen will provide your daily dress requirements, activities and schedule. Red lights will flash in your house alerting you to a new screen message. If you do not follow the directives - you will be punished.

"You will always address each other as Karen and Dee Dee. If you do not - you will be punished."

She watched as her dolls struggled to walk up and down the exercise room, a task made difficult by the tight dresses and unforgiving plastic high heels.

"You will be required to engage in various sexual acts, both by yourself and with each other. If you do not - you will be punished.

"Given the nature of our relationship, you can well imagine the variety of punishments I can inflict. You might well wish to die, to end it all, but *that* will not happen. Resign to your fate, adapt and endure. Welcome to your new home and new life." Elena rose and left.

When Karen turned to walk down the room she saw the elapsed time counter on the screen. *Forty five more minutes of this, then what?*

True to her word, when the on-screen counter ran down to 00:00, red lights flashed. When they finally stopped flashing a new message appeared. FEEDING TIME. REMOVE YOUR GLOVES: 15:00. As Karen and Dwight watched, the timer counted down: 14:59, 14:58…

Dee Dee turned, her feet shuffling in the plastic shoes. "Karen, it looks like we've got less than fifteen minutes to get to the kitchen to eat."

The refrain 'you will be punished' resounded in Karen's head. "Yea, Dee Dee," the derision in his voice was obvious, "let's go."

Elena laughed to see them perilously navigate the stairwell in their tight dresses and high heels. *It won't be long; in one month they'll swish about like the mini-drag-queens they will become.*

Karen nearly stumbled near the end of the stairs. "Fuck this shit!" She rubbed the back of her shoe on the stair until it flew off and fell to the floor below.

Elena's voice stopped their descent. "You do not remove items of clothing until instructed. No hot water for a week, and you WILL bathe and shower every day."

They reached the bottom of the stairs and as Dee Dee helped Karen with her shoe she whispered, "Do you think she'll always be watching?"

Karen shrugged, "Probably not, but I'd bet my ass

we're always being monitored, recorded, whatever. Hell, it's what I'd do. For now we play along, no sense making it hard on ourselves, and in the meantime we'll look for a way out."

Dee Dee stood and helped steady Karen, "I hear what you're saying, but right now…"

Karen nodded. *Right now it seems like Elena has the upper hand., if we can only hold out...*

Elena was right. Their *food* was far from appetizing, not necessarily bad, but definitely bland. For them, eating would no longer be a joyful experience, but rather a biological imperative. There were no plates, silverware or glassware; instead they scooped up handfuls of the gray-green gruel from their feeding trough and slurped it from their palms. Water flowed from a small tube and this they also slurped up by the handful.

Dee Dee had to admit she was impressed with the miniature world Elena had created for them: a world no doubt run by microprocessors and miniature electronics, not to mention all the intricately crafted-to-scale furniture in their 'doll' house. She stifled a laugh. *I bet our own money paid for this.* She chuckled at the irony.

The red lights flashed and they looked at the screen. CLEAN THE TROUGH WITH YOUR HANDS. Suddenly a torrent of water rushed through the trough and they used their hands to scrub and wipe up traces of the gruel as the water washed it away.

They cleaned the trough until the red lights once more flashed and a new message appeared. PREPARE FOR BED. GO TO THE BEDROOM. PUT ON PINK NIGHTGOWNS. HOLD HANDS. 15:00, 14:59…

The two living dolls stared at the message and subconsciously their hands sought one another. Hand-in-hand they negotiated the stairwell and made their way to the bedroom. In the bedroom they helped each other remove the dresses and put away their hats gloves and shoes. They rummaged through the dresser, found two pink nightgowns and slipped them on. They waited.

The lights slowly dimmed and they saw the last message of the day: GO TO BED. NO TALKING. Silently, they slipped into their one bed and pulled the covers around them.

Elena smiled as each of her dolls moved to the edge of the bed, creating a vacant spot in the center, the homophobic reaction of being in bed with another man. *That will change. They will change.*

The red lights flashed again, but Karen was already awake. She hadn't slept much and rose up on her forearm and looked out the glass wall. KAREN: BATH, DEE DEE: SHOWER. She felt Dwight tumble from the bed. *Not Dwight, Dee Dee.*

The two of them padded into the bathroom and found the water running in the shower and the bathtub. Small, doll-sized towels were on a shelf.

Karen put her hand in the bath water and quickly pulled it out. "Shit! That stuff's freezin'!"

Dee Dee tentatively reached into the shower and pulled her hand back. "Mine too, she did say that we wouldn't have warm water for a week."

Elena's voice prodded them to action. "You must each spend ten minutes in the water. If you do not, the cold water lasts for an additional week - and you will have visitors tonight."

Karen stepped into the tub, the chilling water coming up to mid calf. Dee Dee watched and stepped into her shower.

"All the way in" Elena said, "the timer won't start until you are immersed."

Both dolls slipped into their respective waters, their sharp gasps of breath testament to the cold water assaulting their skin.

As Karen settled into the bathtub she saw the timer start: 10;00, 9:59, 9:58. She closed her eyes and shook, splashing water over the sides.

Dee Dee was huddled under the shower spray, her hands clutched around her violently shaking body.

The shower stopped and the water started draining from the bathtub when the red lights flashed. DRY OFF. PUT TOWELS IN CHUTE. FEED. They saw a blinking light over a small hole and pushed the towels inside; a vacuumed *WHOOSH* quickly pulling them away.

Karen and Dee Dee looked at each other, and silently walked downstairs to the feeding trough. Both men were educated, trained scientists, and recognized the protocols of operant conditioning. How long could they hold out before... Before the lights and screen commands were unnecessary.

They ate their gruel and slurped their water. When prompted, they washed the trough with their hands. The next command seemed easy enough: GO TO LIVING ROOM. SIT. HOLD HANDS. WATCH VIDEO.

Hand-in-hand they walked to the living room and sat on the floral couch. They moved apart, so their naked bodies weren't touching, but they still held hands. *You never know when SHE'S watching.*

They stared at the real world, so far removed from them beyond the glass. Suddenly the LCD screen flickered to life. For the next hour they watched a video on women's fashion and style. Or at least they attempted to watch; it was hard for both of them to stay focused on a continual discourse color, fabric and style. *Where is she going with all of this?* When the video finally ended it was hard for them to remember what they had watched and how to put it in context? *What next?* They didn't have to wait long. GO TO YOUR BEDROOM. PUT ON WORKOUT CLOTHES.

Karen stood before the bedroom dresser, "What are workout clothes?"

Dee Dee rummaged through a drawer and pulled out spandex tights and a short spandex crop top, both were lavender, "Something like this."

As Dee Dee wiggled into her outfit Karen fished a similar outfit in pink from the drawers.

Both dolls helped each other tug and pull the skintight clothes into place.

"This is fuckin' bullshit," Karen groused.

"Shhh, she might hear you!" Dee Dee excitedly looked around, as if Elena might appear from anywhere.

The red lights flashed and the two immediately looked at the screen, as if to receive divine guidance from their electronic god. GO TO EXERCISE ROOM. FOLLOW VIDEO.

In bare feet they padded to the exercise room and waited. Again, the screen flickered and a Yoga video began. For the next ninety minutes the two struggled to complete a beginner's Yoga class.

Elena laughed as she watched both Karen and Dee Dee struggle with Downward Dog. *They'll adapt, a few weeks of Yoga, Pilates, Aerobics, and Pole Dance Classes will achieve what I want.* She watched as Karen stood and started to walk away.

Her fingers stabbed at her phone. "You must follow all directives, failure to comply means punishment."

Dee Dee and Karen froze in place, their eyes darting, looking for their captor, her voice a constant reminder of their submission. She watched Karen curse, but walk back to her place and attempt to master Warrior One position.

By the end of their workout, her dolls were sweaty and tired, but Elena had prepared for that. Their existence for the next few days was pre-programmed into a computer server: when they slept, ate, bathed, what they did, and what they wore. Their cute Lycra workout clothes were stained with dark blotches of sweat and they wiped the sweat from their face with their hands. Their heads turned to the glass wall as the red lights flashed: CHANGE YOUR CLOTHES. PUT ON NIGHTGOWNS. NAP.

Karen and Dee Dee trudged to their bedroom, put on their nightgowns and crawled into bed. The lights slowly dimmed. Dee Dee turned to face Karen and whispered, "Is it night? I mean - I know she dimmed the lights, but - I've lost track of time, day and night."

"Yea," Karen muttered. "It's her way of demonstrating her total control, upset our circadian rhythms."

"What can we do?" Dee Dee received no reply, only the stirring as Karen pulled the covers over her.

For the next few days the cycle was the same, to mean random, chaotic. Feeding times were never the same, not that they had the capacity to track time. Elena had been thorough in removing any clocks or other devices that recorded time, day, date, night or day. Their reality was what she made it.

They watched and performed to endless exercise and dance videos, dressed and practiced walking, and had their twice daily feedings at the trough. Elena displayed the cockroach cage on a shelf across the room, clearly visible to them, and she made a show of feeding the gruesome bugs and teasing them about 'joining in on the feedings.'

Karl didn't know how Dee Dee felt, but he was glad that Elena seemed to hold back on the 'Lesbian/sex thing' she'd originally alluded to. Other than the initial kiss there had only been the usual hand-holding as the two dolls moved about the house. His relief turned to panic on the third day. He and Dee Dee sat holding hands on the sofa, waiting for the video they were instructed to watch.

His worst fears were realized when the large, flat screen television flickered to life. It was an instructional video: *How to Perform Fellatio*. It was hosted by a well known porn star and featured several hot women and two very well hung men.

Karl ripped his hand from Dee Dee's. "Fuck this shit!" His eyes scanned the room for the hundredth time, looking for some sign of escape or defense against their captor and, for the hundredth time, found none.

Dee Dee reached out and took his hand. "Karen!

She might be watching, listening, recording, and remember…" Dee Dee's free hand pointed to the roaches.

The two living dolls sat back and watched the forty-five minute video, wondering if they'd later be forced to demonstrate the techniques to their captor's satisfaction. The video ended and the message display read: WAIT.

Again the screen flickered to life and another video, *Guys on Guys* started. This one was all male, featuring a host of oral and anal exploits. Karl turned away often, but Dee Dee managed to watch uninterrupted, which made Karl worry.

Their luxury of being couch potatoes was at an end when the final screen message directed them back upstairs to practice erotic dance. They were directed to exchange their long gowns for sexy fringed bras and short-shorts, but kept the long gloves and high heels on.

Elena entered halfway through their dance practice. She sat in a chair and watched as they followed the moves and gyrations of the dancers in the video, twisting and rolling their hips, tracing lines down their body and initiating sexy 'come hither' movements with their hands. She laughed, especially at Karl/Karen. *Such a male asshole before, and now look at him!* She supposed she should feel pity for them, but Karl had always been a misogynist ass, and Dwight was a gutless follower. *The world, at least the world of women, is better off without them.*

"You are adjusting well?" she asked. Her voice held no concern whether they were or not.

They both nodded, perspiration glistening on their doll-sized bodies.

Elena leaned towards the glass to get a closer look

at them. "In the future you will answer with a curtsey and a 'yes, Goddess' or 'no, Goddess'." She stood, towering over them and their dollhouse prison in her four inch heels. "Am I not a Goddess to you?"

Karen stood open mouthed as Dee Dee curtsied and said 'Yes, Goddess'.

Elena showed no signs of pleasure or displeasure; rather she nodded and left the room. She didn't have to be present to control every detail of their lives.

"What's with the fuckin' bowing stuff, Dwight?"

"It's a curtsey, my sister had to learn to do 'em when we were kids. And I'm Dee Dee."

Dee Dee was spared Karen's outrage by the latest message: NAKED. FEED. 15:00. Both dolls stripped off their clothes and ran to the kitchen feeding trough.

The day dawned bright and sunny for Elena. Whether it was day or night, her living dolls didn't know, may never know. Before leaving for work she spent time in her office, programming the day's activities for her subjects; a few keystrokes were all that were required to control the existence of two hapless males. Among the day's training she had planned was an old instruction video she had found on performing curtsies. She'd had it digitized and programmed it to run three times that day, with a fifteen minute practice session following each viewing.

The blinking lights stirred the dolls from their

slumber and both padded barefoot from their bed. Clad only in their pink baby doll pajamas they stumbled to the glass wall, dreading to learn their fates for the day. Karen groaned at the first message, it didn't bode well for the future. NAKED. FEED. HOLD EACH OTHER'S COCKS.

Karen was still staring at the message display when she felt Dee Dee grab her cock. As if Elena had anticipated his hesitancy the next message was: DO NOT DISOBEY. Karen ruefully reached his right hand over and felt for Dee Dee's cock. Cocks-in-hand the dolls walked to their trough to feed.

They'd become inured to their feeding ritual, scooping up the gruel with their hands, lapping up the water and cleaning the trough. Elena was providing sustenance, but no pleasure or enjoyment in the process. They dried their hands and dropped the tiny towels into a chute. They were always provided with clean clothes and towels. *At least we don't have to do fuckin' laundry*, Karl thought.

The flashing lights brought them back to the transparent wall that revealed the world outside, but kept it forever out of reach. EXERCISE. YOGA. They turned to walk to the upstairs dance and exercise room when Karen felt Dee Dee grab his cock.

"She didn't tell us to stop holding cocks," Dee Dee said. "I mean…"

Karen sighed and grabbed Dee Dee's cock as well. *Dwight's fucked; she's broken him. I'm on my own here.*

Having no instructions to dress, they performed their ninety minute Yoga workout in the nude.

Elena looked at her watch and pulled out her

expensive and very high-tech cell phone. She punched the necessary buttons and was quickly rewarded with a video display on her phone. She punched the '+' button and zoomed in on her naked Yoga practitioners. She smiled as she watched them assume the triangle pose, their cocks dangling between their legs. *The pride and the downfall of the male.* She punched another button and raised the phone to make a call.

Elena's voice filled the house, "You will bathe when you are finished with your exercise. Each of you will use the depilatory cream on the other's body. Once you are clean, hairless and smooth you will be fed."

Dee Dee glanced at the timer, another twenty seven minutes of Yoga. Her eyes stopped for a moment on Karen's cock, but she quickly looked away when Karen scowled at her.

Elena dropped her briefcase on the hall table and relaxed on her couch. She'd spend a few minutes review-ing some critical items before she took her dolls to the next level. With the remote she quickly called up selected video feeds of the day's activities. Her dolls assiduously went through their regime for the day: exercise, dressing up, catwalk model practice, erotic dance class, watching sexual instruction videos. Elena particularly noted how easily Dee Dee reached over to take Karen's hand. *Dee Dee's ready. It will take longer for Karl to become Karen, but eventually...*

She changed the display from recorded video to

'live', and watched as her dolls engaged in high heel practice. For thirty five minutes they'd been wearing high heels, the only footwear available to them, and walking up and down their exercise room. The goal was simple: maintain correct posture, sway the hips, keep the hands limp, and cross one foot over the other, staying directly on the pink line running the length of the room. For the exercise duration, today it was forty five minutes, they'd walk to one end of the room, turn and dip, walk to the other end, turn and dip, endlessly.

Elena had scoured flea markets and on-line sources to obtain a vast collection of fashion-doll-sized shoes. These had been meticulously modified and enhanced to work on a real, albeit scaled-to-doll-sized person. In the few days that they'd become her perpetual prisoners, her dolls were beginning to get used to high heels. *When you haven't got a choice – and when you get LOTS of practice. Hmmm, a drop of super glue in each shoe, slide them on, and voila! A permanently high heeled doll.*

She pressed the 'mic' button on the remote, "When the exercise ends you will feed and then wait for me, naked, in your bedroom."

It always amused her to see them jump at the sound of her voice, but they never knew when she would appear, either in person or as a disembodied ethereal voice. She'd stripped them of privacy, power, control and knowledge. *Next to go, their heterosexual proclivities.*

They heard and felt her before they ever saw her, the sound of a door closing, footfalls on stairs, the vibration of movement transmitted to their doll house. It was obvious someone was entering their environment, and they'd never seen anyone other than Elena.

She paused and went to the far side of the room, and they watched as she dropped lettuce leaves into the roach's cage and give it a slight shake. The sudden flurry of insect activity caused a shudder among both dolls.

"You seem to have been very obedient today." Elena smiled, noting that they sat, naked on the edge of their bed, still holding each other's cock. "Come closer, to the wall."

She leaned close to examine them as they flattened themselves against the transparent wall. "Yes, you seem healthy enough. Any problems to report?"

Dee Dee quickly dropped into her curtsey and replied, "No, Goddess."

Karen paused, obviously the habit not yet fully ingrained, and executed a sloppy curtsey. "No, Goddess."

Her exquisitely manicured nail tapped the glass in front of Karen. "That was sloppy and half-hearted." She turned to Dee Dee, "You're doing well, but it still needs improvement."

Dee Dee followed with another curtsey, "Yes, Goddess."

Elena silently eyed the two. *Karl can't last much longer, especially with Dee Dee so compliant.* "Until the curtsies are up to standard you will maintain the same three times a day video viewing and practice sessions. From now on you are to wear petticoats to practice. Your goal is a perfect curtsey, deep, with outstretched arms holding billowing petticoats, smoothly executed with a big smile. Understood?"

Both curtsied in unison this time, "Yes, Goddess."

"And now," Elena paused, "let's discuss your sex

lives – with each other." She noted Dee Dee's blank look, *not unexpected, she'll comply*, and Karen's look of rage and loathing. "You will have sex with each other," she sat back in her chair, "first to please and amuse me. But eventually," her lips curled into a devious smile, "because it will be one of the few pleasures and enjoyments available to you. Hold each other's cocks."

She watched as Dee Dee quickly grabbed Karen's, and Karen grudgingly took hold of Dee Dee's.

"You watched the instructional today, and you'll see it, and many more, repeatedly as you are trained to be sexual performers." She leaned in, wanting to get a good look. "Squeeze the cock in your hand, feel it." Her eyes focused on the tiny hands grabbing the miniature cocks. "Does it feel good? Use your other hand to stroke it."

Karen suddenly yelled and backed up, her hands flying away from Dee Dee's crotch. "Shit! You're gettin' hard; what are you a fuckin' fag?"

Elena had to keep from laughing; a humorous tone now might degrade the training about to take place. "What she was feeling, Karen, was pleasure at being touched. You two are alone, and will be, you're going to have to depend on each other. The quicker you accept your existence, and your new sexuality, the better off you will be."

Karen stood, hands at her sides, her fists clenched, scared and angry.

"I know this particular part of your training is going to be difficult," Elena's voice had a softer, motherly tone. "Dee Dee, I want you to kneel and kiss Karen's cock. No sucking, just the foreplay as you saw in the video." Her voice took an edge, "Karen, you are to let her do whatever I say, relax, don't fight it."

Dee Dee knelt and took Karen's cock in her hands, stroked it and licked the head.

Elena watched two contradictory actions, Karen gnashing her teeth in a grimace of disgust and her tiny cock beginning to swell. She nodded her approval, "Dee Dee, do what you learned from the video."

Dee Dee ran her tongue up and down Karen's fleshy shaft, her tongue gave quick kitten-licks to the head of the cock, then she ran her tongue in circles around the head.

"Very nice," Elena said. "Put it in your mouth Dee Dee, start sucking. Relax, Karen, cum if you want. Your existence won't allow you many pleasures; sex will be one of the few. I could have had those *things* removed. I've allowed you to keep them because I expect you to use them."

Dee Dee was trying, but was clearly a neophyte and struggled to get her mouth around Karen's swelling cock.

"It's not necessary to take it all today, Dee Dee, just make Karen feel good. Eventually I *will* expect both of you to deep throat, but there'll be time and practice, LOTS of practice for you to achieve that."

Karen's eyes were closed, but her face was conflicted with revulsion and pleasure. While her mind reeled at the homosexual act her biology betrayed her with an impressive erection.

"Obviously the minimizing procedure hasn't affected that," observed Elena as she watched Karen's cock grow in Dee Dee's mouth. "See, you both still contribute to our scientific research in your own *little* way."

Dee Dee's hands cupped and massaged Karen's

balls and when Dee Dee's fingers flicked around her puckered opening, Karen lost it.

Karen's hands grabbed Dee Dee's head and pulled the kneeling doll hard into her crotch. Karen pumped her ass as her cock discharged repeatedly into Dee Dee's warm and inviting mouth.

When Karen pulled her cock from her housemate's hungry lips, Dee Dee stayed close, her tongue lapping up the vestiges of living-doll cum. Karen didn't protest, rather she let her kneeling friend lick and nuzzle the cock as it lowered to rest.

Elena beamed, "Very well done, girls. Normally I'd expect Karen to reciprocate," she noted the now wide-eyed expression on Karen's face, "but not this evening." She cast a stern look at Karen, "You will learn to be down on your knees, pleasing each other, and when those skills are fully developed," she watched them turn to her, "you'll complete your sexual odyssey." She chuckled at their confused expressions, "You'll fuck each other in the ass, girls. You'll suck each other's cocks. I left you those little things and housed you here, in a feminized doll-house environment, so you could be my little playthings, my mini lesbians. Welcome home sluts."

END?

"How are we doing down there?" Patricia purred. Her honeyed tones couldn't disguise the malevolence in her voice. Her hands reached between his legs and pulled his shriveled cock from its ice water bath.

"Jeez! It's so tiny and wrinkled," Heather mocked.

Monique crinkled her nose, "Yecchh, put it back in."

Patricia held the wrinkled flesh between her thumb and first finger and shook her head. "Yes, it *is* disgusting." She slapped it, "And QUITE fucking useless, which is why we're locking it up."

Locked Away

"He doesn't look happy." Monique ran her fingers around the rim of her wine glass. Her nails nearly matched the color of the expensive Merlot. "Are you happy?"

Drake imperceptibly nodded; he could scarce do otherwise. He was bound, kneeling on a small raised platform on the coffee table before the three women. His thighs were spread wide, his cock and balls dangling below. The stiff posture collar also secured the wrist cuffs fastened behind his neck. A steel bar ran from the rear of the posture collar to the coffee table, rendering him immobile. The ball gag in his mouth prevented any intelligible response.

Patricia, his Wife/Mistress had secured him to his place of honor an hour ago, long before her guests arrived.

Heather reached over to refill Monique's glass. "I don't know why you even ask if he's comfortable; just teasing I suppose. I mean – really – a slave? Comfort-able?" Heather was the youngest, perhaps the cruelest of the three. Today she wore a slim black pencil skirt and a white blouse, shamelessly unbuttoned to display her impressive décolletage. A mane of blonde hair cascaded to her shoulders and framed a pretty cheerleader, girl-next-door face. Her eyes were ice blue and held no warmth, not for any male.

Patricia stood, noting how Drake's eyes followed her every move. Her fingers delicately traced a line around his ball gag, and she smiled as she watched him inhale the scent of her fragrance.

His eyes grew wider as he watched those exqui-site fingers lower, poised over his nipples. He flinched as she flicked at the clothespins on his nipples, the 'thwack-thwack' of blood red nails on a wooden clothes-pin seeming to echo in the room.

Patricia smiled as each flick of her finger made her sub-hubby jolt.

"Gawd, Pat, you love tormenting the little slut don't you?" Heather leaned back in her chair and crossed her legs. She knew the rustle of her nylons and her dangling high heel would torment Drake in their own ways.

"We both love it, don't we babykins?" Patricia stopped flicking the clothespin and now began twisting them – slowly. She bent down and kissed his nose, leaving a crimson imprint of her sensuous lips. She was the oldest of the group, their founder and leader. Today she was dressed in a knee-length gray dress, a black patent belt cinching her tiny waist and emphasizing her womanly curves. Soft brown hair fell to her shoulders and her eyes were the color of aged Cognac.

He moaned through the gag when she pulled off the clothespins. The blood flowed back into the distressed area, a new rush of pain.

His wife was not to end his torment, not now. Not ever? The vicious clothespins were quickly attached to his earlobes, earrings of agony for the captive and submissive male. Hers was the gift to inflict continuous and varied torments, a skill she was intent to pass on to her eager acolytes.

Heather and Monique exchanged knowing glances. Their friend, Patricia, certainly had things well in hand. She was their mentor, and with her guidance they would form the nucleus of the Brent-Haven Women's Auxiliary, an organization with a decidedly different agenda. Today was Drake's Chastity Day, an event that lay ominously in the future of Heather and Monique's husbands.

"How are we doing down there?" Patricia purred. Her feigned concern couldn't disguise the malevolence in her voice. Her hands reached between his legs and pulled his shriveled cock from its ice water bath.

"Jeez! It's so tiny and wrinkled," Heather mocked.

Monique crinkled her nose, "Yecchh, put it back in."

Patricia held the wrinkled flesh between her thumb and first finger and shook her head. "Yes, it *is* disgusting." She slapped it, "And QUITE fucking useless, which is why we're locking it up." She dropped it back in the ice water bath and unceremoniously covered it with more ice cubes from a nearby ice bucket.

She packed the ice around his frigid and shrunken cock, giving no concerns to his moans and pleas from behind his gag. "It needs to be small, as small as I can get it," she laughed. "I had his device made quite small; there won't be the remotest chance of any kind of erection."

"And his last time, "Monique asked, "how was that?" Monique was the tallest of the three, and the most beautiful. At five ten she was an imposing six three in her five inch heels. Today she was dressed in black slacks and a gray sweater that showed off her assets. It was her height, and super model looks, that made her a hit on the catwalk. She'd left that behind, but not the need to be an object of desire, or to have men fall at her feet.

"Did he cry or beg?" Heather asked.

Patricia added more ice water to the cock bath and the women laughed as Drake squirmed and gasped. She slapped his face, "Be still! His last squirt of that disgusting sissy cream was last Thursday, wasn't it Drakeywakey?" She talked baby talk as she pinched and pulled on his tender nipples. "Mummy and my younger sister came over, didn't they snookums?" Patricia handed Monique a small photo album, "We took pictures."

"He's so cute in that pink party dress," Monique gushed. She showed the pictures to Heather.

"Such a lovely sissy," Heather mocked.

Patricia nodded like a proud mother, "He served tea and refreshments."

Heather's eyes were slits as she stared at Drake. "Damn, I can't wait until my own Tony is in a dress, waiting on me hand and foot."

Patricia added more ice cubes to her hapless slave's cock bath, not that it would increase his suffering, but simply because she could. "He had to kneel and beg my mother and my sister to be allowed to masturbate. It was extremely humiliating for him, precisely the point." She moved the clothespins from his ears, back to his nipples, a traveling parade of pain about his body. "They made him crawl, bark like a dog, lick their shoes. My sister threw food on the floor, crushed it and made him eat it off the bottom of her shoe. It was such fun to watch. Finally they let him play with Mr. Cockywocky, didn't they precious?" she tweaked his nose. "Mother made him cum on her shoes and then lick it off. I have pictures – and video."

Monique's eyes lit up, "I like THAT! Roger's always giving me shit about buying shoes. Well, soon he'll be on his knees worshipping every single pair."

The ladies raised their glasses in a regal toast to Female Domination.

Patricia placed her empty glass on the table. "Yes, the piercings have healed, the device has been sized, ordered and received; he's had his last orgasm and," she pulled his frigid and withered cock from its ice bath, "I do believe our little slut is ready."

He was on his hands and knees, his eyes focused on the alluring legs before him, clad in expensive sheer, seamed stockings, and ending in three pair of expensive and dangerous looking stilettos. His Mistress reached down and clipped a leash to his collar.

A silent tug on the leash had him crawling behind the three pair of superior feminine legs and shoes. The menacing clicks of the spike heels on the tile floor were in sharp contrast to the plodding of his knees and fleshy palms on that same floor.

They stopped in the kitchen, at the refrigerator. Patricia opened the door and removed a silver serving tray; nestled on a bed of pink and purple tufted velvet lay his chastity device.

"Wow," Monique tapped it with her fingernail, "it's *really* small." An evil smile crossed her face, "Shit! To be able to lock Roger up in something like that…"

Heather nudged Drake's naked thigh with the pointed toe of her stiletto, "Has he seen it?"

"No," Patricia tugged on his leash, bringing him to heel, "he was measured for it, but doesn't know anything else about it, do you?"

Drake shook his head, with the gag still in place he was reduced to non-verbal responses.

"Up!" commanded Patricia as she pulled on his leash.

He stood, but kept his head bowed, eyes on the floor. Constant face slappings and 'what the FUCK are you looking at' recriminations quickly developed the necessary submissive postures in him.

"We need to work quickly, while everything is still cold," Patricia advised. She took a tube of cooled lubricant from the refrigerator and lubed his shrunken cock. "Congeals a bit when chilled, but his body temperature will get it going. Goodness!" she mocked, "it's so tiny it uses hardly any lube."

"Can I remove his PA piercing?" Heather asked.

"Go ahead," Patricia said. "We're using a new high-tech one in its place, something *very* secure."

He stood, mute, eyes cast to the floor as Patricia and her friends molested his private parts.

Monique whispered in his ear, "Better enjoy it bitch, it might be the last time you feel anything human down there."

"Look up slut," barked Patricia.

He looked up to see her holding the device: two short inches of gleaming medical stainless steel, slightly curved and tapered. The end was finished in a web of cutouts, the cage framing his flesh in a 'stained glass' chastity motif. The device struck fear into him, although he had to admire the obvious quality and craftsmanship that had gone into it.

"Yes," Patricia said, "it gets smaller toward the end, although it isn't very big in the first place. I love the cage work at the end, where he can see glimpses of it locked away."

"No shit," Heather said, "it looks expensive."

"Oh it was!" laughed Patricia, "look at the workmanship, the materials, my little sweetums will have $15,000 worth of hardware between his legs."

"Get out!" Monique leaned in to get a closer look "for that?"

Patricia nodded, "Custom sized, custom made, with several unique high tech enhancements."

Heather waved her right foot, rotating it on the stiletto heel, the wicked pointed toe making lazy arcs in the air. "Still, that's a shitload of money to spend on a slave."

Patricia shrugged, "I sold his truck, those expensive golf clubs, his boat, there was enough money for the device and some pretty maid uniforms as well."

Monique clapped her hands, "I think my Roger can raise the money, but *I'm* keeping his Porsche."

Patricia held the device next to Drake's miniscule cock, "Yes ladies, chilling the cock is essential; it goes in small…"

"And stays small!" they all laughed in unison.

"This hand-cuff like piece," Patricia said as she playfully opened and closed it, "goes behind the balls."

"This is so exciting," Monique said.

"Yes," Heather agreed, "it's nice of you to invite us to his – uh – *little* ceremony."

Patricia positioned the device at the head of Drake's cock. "The first of many," she laughed, "this will be the official coming out party for all those new males inducted into our group. Ready?"

Ready or not, Drake felt the fine feminine fingers work his chilled cock into the icy metal tube. He was surprised at how easily he fit into the device. *Am I really that small?*

"Say 'bye-bye'," Monique laughed.

Patricia's hands partially closed the ring around his balls. She looked at Heather, "Remove his gag."

Drake breathed in Heather's scent as her fingers worked at the buckle behind his neck. *They're cruel, but they always smell so nice.*

In her five inch heels Patricia towered over the cowering and flat-footed Drake. She bent down, coming eye to eye with him. "Beg me to close the ring and lock it."

All three women closed in on him, watching,

listening; he had no choice but to comply. "Please, Mistress Patricia, please lock away my worthless cock."

"Oh, gawd," purred Monique, "I love it when they get all submissive and pitiful."

"Is that the best you can do, really?" Patricia pinched and twisted his nipple, smiling as she watched him writhe from her torment. "C'mon, really beg; make me want to lock you up."

"Please, Mistress, please lock away my worthless cock. It's useless to pleasure a woman, and if you lock it up I won't be tempted to play with it."

Patricia gently stroked his cheek, "See you can do it when you try."

Heather and Monique giggled, amused by the way Patricia easily manipulated her slave/husband.

"Since you asked so nicely," Patricia's fingers closed the ring with a 'click'. She tested the fit, "I think we can go another." She closed the ring with another 'click.' "Almost there, one more," she teased. With a final click she released her hand.

Monique and Heather took the opportunity to inspect the device, hefting its weight in their hand and pulling on it to check the fitting of the ball ring.

"This last ring secures it in the front, through his PA piercing." Patricia held up a small silver ring.

"That's it?" asked Monique.

"Far from it," sneered Patricia. "Look closely; see those little teeth on one end? When I close the ring they interlock with similar teeth on the inside. It can't be pulled apart."

Heather nodded her approval, "So it's permanent?"

"No, the designer made sure that one set of teeth is movable, they can be retracted out of the way and the ring can be opened." Patricia smiled, proud of the new toy for her pet, "There's supposedly a special tool with Neodymium magnets that fits over the ring and the magnets line up with one set of magnetized teeth and the tool causes the teeth to retract and the ring can be opened. Or something like that, it's all very technical."

Monique leaned in for a closer look, "All in there? It's so small."

"Yes," Patricia said, that's one of the reasons the device was so expensive, the technology and hand work that went into it. I mean, the device to unlock the new PA ring costs fifteen hundred dollars."

"Fifteen hundred? Sounds like a LOT of money to me," Heather said.

"Oh, I quite agree," Patricia held the ring in front of Drake's eyes, "that's why I didn't buy it." She saw the look of terror in Drake's eyes and felt a flood of warmth flow through her.

"You didn't buy it?" asked Monique and Heather in unison.

Patricia bent down and began to work the new ring through the device and Drake's PA piercing. "No, I saw this lovely pair of shoes and got those instead. If I ever need the device to remove the ring, the maker of the chastity belt said that he can make one for me, shouldn't take more than – two months."

Patricia stood, once again towering over her sub-missive husband. She held the ring, now threaded through his cock and the device, between her fingers. "Once I close this, the teeth engage, and it won't come off. It's quite resistant to tampering and cutting, with conventional tools. I'm afraid any unauthorized attempts at removal would involve significant collateral damage."

The women were all focused on Drake's eyes, drinking in every nuance of fear, submission, terror and hopelessness.

"Beg for it, beg me to close the ring," Patricia ordered.

His own voice sounded detached to him, as if someone else was speaking, "Please secure the device Mistress, I'm not worthy to have an erection and cum. Please lock me away."

Click by click Patricia sealed his fate. "Secure, but not damaging," she said. She pointed to the larger cuff ring behind his balls. "This ring actually has a built-in lock, a special one-of-a-kind lock made by the belt's designer," she handed keys to Monique and Heather. "We each have a key, although it only unlocks the ball ring, his PA ring still secures the front on the device."

"And you didn't order the tool to release *that*!" Heather laughed.

"No," agreed Patricia, "I'd have to special order that, so he's still several weeks away from a release, even if we wanted to release him."

"Which we don't," Monique mocked.

Drake visibly winced at each cutting remark by the women.

Monique looked at the key in her hand, "So…do we really *need* these keys? I mean…"

"Yea," chirped Heather.

Patricia walked around her husband, circling him, her stilettos clicking on the floor, her fingernails tracing a line around his naked midsection as she stalked her prey. "Do we, darling? Do we need these keys? Are you going to want out? Ever? Hmmm?" She slapped his face, "Speak!"

"N – n – no, Mistress. There's no need for me to be released – ever."

"Well then ladies," Patricia smiled, "let's resolve Drake's little dilemma, shall we?" She jerked Drake's leash and pulled him forward, to the garage.

The concrete floor was cool to Drake's bare feet. Wordlessly he followed as Patricia led him to the garage workbench.

Each woman made a show of placing her key on the work bench.

"We want to keep the keys, we're each going to start a charm bracelet, made up of the keys to the chastity devices of sniveling, submissive males," Patricia explained.

"Yes," Monique said, "but there's no reason for those keys to be functional. We don't want males to think there's any hope of relief."

"Exactly," Heather added, "whenever a male sees that bracelet, with all those keys, he'll know his place, his fate, the hopelessness of his situation."

"So," Patricia picked up one of the keys and handed it to Drake, "put the key in the vise and file off the teeth, nice and smooth."

"And totally useless," Heather laughed.

Drake took the key and secured it in the vise. Patricia handed him a file and the ladies watched as he filed away the teeth, rendering the key useless and ensuring his permanent chastity.

"Make sure it's smooth, then kneel and present it to Monique," Patricia ordered.

Drake ran his finger over the key, looking for sharp edges or burrs. He touched up two places, checked again for smoothness, and finally removed the key. He turned and knelt, his knees kissing the cool concrete floor. With outstretched hands he made his offering, "Please accept this key, Mistress Monique."

She smiled as she held out her palm and felt the key fall into it. "The first of many, I'm going to love the sound of jangling keys on my wrist."

Within minutes Drake had rendered the other two keys useless as well, kneeling and presenting them in turn to Heather and Patricia.

"You know," Patricia's eyes scanned the workbench until she found what she was looking for, "since the keys are useless, we may as well go all the way." She reached up and pulled down a tube of epoxy from the pegboard, taking a moment to read the package, "Super-strength and fast-setting." She thrust the epoxy at Drake, "Mix this up."

The women exchanged knowing glances as Drake silently mixed the two components. If he'd thought this was all happenstance he was mistaken. The day's activities had been carefully planned and choreographed by his three antagonists.

"Hurry," Patricia ordered, "before it sets. Fill in that lock. Even if there was a key, or we happened to get a duplicate, we don't want it to be used – do we?"

"No, Mistress." Drake used a plastic applicator to work the epoxy deeply into the lock's mechanism. He finally discarded the applicator and used a rag to wipe away any remaining epoxy.

Patricia grabbed the chastity device and used it to turn Drake to face the two women. She inspected the special locking PA ring and the ball ring, its lock now filled with epoxy and its keys rendered useless. "That's the proper condition for a submissive male," she said, "locked away."

END

Susan lit her cigarette and smoked in silence.
"Open." She said it in a simple, everyday fashion, confident that a properly trained male would respond. And he
did, tilting his head back and opening his mouth wide.
She leaned forward to blow smoke in his face and tapped
an ash into the waiting mouth. A smile crossed her lips
as he dutifully swallowed the ash and opened his mouth
for yet another.

A Visit To Smythe Stables

*L*ike the others in the pens, he heard her before he saw her. The first thing to meet his eyes were the gleaming black boots, long pointed toes and wicked spiked heels.

Life in the pens was a meager existence, but the presence of one of the warders always increased the unpleasantness factor; better to be alone - forgotten.

The click-clacking of the stilettos on the concrete floor stopped, replaced by the ominous slapping of a crop against a leather boot.

"We'll have visitors today, you like visitors don't you?" Her pleasant voice didn't disguise her contempt. "Something to perk up your drab existence?"

The stock in the pens knelt on the hard, cold floor. They shuddered and silently grimaced. Visitors were bad, there was no such thing as a good visit. The agony of solitary confinement was preferable to any visit.

The slapping of the crop grew louder. "I'll expect all of you to be obedient, compliant," the warder laughed, the echo reverberating from pen to pen, "and very pro-ductive."

The gravel crunched under the tires as the black and white chartered bus, its tinted windows hiding the occupants inside, made its way up the winding drive. It passed a green fenced in pasture and a wooded area as it slowed to a stop in front of the imposing red and white building. It was a long low and windowless structure with several sliding doors along one side; the sign in the front, Smythe Stables, was the only clue as to what might be inside. With a hiss, the doors of the bus folded open.

A tall austere woman rose from her seat at the front of the bus and turned to face her young charges. Her height was enhanced by the gleaming black stilettos, and the long, sheer nylon covered legs that extended from her black leather pencil skirt. She moved effortless-ly on the wicked high heels as she walked down the aisle of the bus. Smiling back at her were row after row of young ladies, this year's graduating class from Lady Caroline's Academy for Young Ladies. "Today is the practical exercise in the milking of the submissive male. We've covered the theory and physiology in the class-room. Here you will put the theory into practice. Your future husbands will need to be regularly milked. Wheth-er or not you do this, or assign it to someone else, it is important to have full knowledge of what is involved in the practice. It is my recommendation that either you, or your Alpha Male lover, perform this service on your husband. Such personal *attention* is more humiliating to the male and drives them further into submission. Ms Constance Pennington Smythe has made her milking stable available to us, very generous of her. When we're finished here she will host an afternoon tea for us at her mansion. Are there any questions?"

A beautiful girl with flowing blonde hair raised her hand. She was dressed in the same uniform as her classmates: a crisp white blouse, sheer stockings, bracelet-length kid leather gloves, a tartan mini skirt and high-heeled court shoes. "Where do all the males inside come from?"

Lady Caroline slipped on her black leather suit coat, "Disciplinary problems, males who couldn't be trained or perform to standards. A few languish here simply because their owners tired of them, and at least here they can serve some function." She turned to look at a pretty brunette. "Susan, I believe your step-father is inside."

Susan smiled and nodded. "Mother sold him to Ms Smythe. He was getting in the way, wasn't good for sex, a premature ejaculator Mom said, and wasn't a good domestic. We have a better sissy maid now, and her new boyfriend, Miguel, is a better lover for Mom."

The girl in the seat in front of Susan turned around. "Your step-dad's in there? That's fuckin' cool."

Her outburst brought instant recrimination from Lady Caroline. "Deidre, mind your language!"

"Yes, Ma'am."

"Remember girls, domination and superiority are

not crass; wield your power and authority in a regal and ladylike manner. When we go inside you will each pick out a slave. Warders will be around to provide you with gloves and lubricant and show you how to hook the suction nipple to their penis. The males have not been milked for several days so should be very amenable to our attention. But to help them along everyone add a spritz of scent."

Twenty five gloved hands disappeared into twenty five identical and fashionable clutches to remove bottles of expensive perfume. In an instant the bus filled with a sensual aroma.

The male bus driver, naked, his mouth filled with a large penis gag, breathed in the heady scent and felt his cock try to stiffen in its chastity cage. The sharp spikes inside the device brought immediate pain and put down any attempts at erection.

Caroline returned to the front of the bus. "When you get inside, remember YOU are the superior Female. This is your last semester at my academy. You're all of legal and marriageable age, and when you graduate you will enter the world to search out and cull those submissive males from the herd. It won't be difficult. Society abounds with them, and I and my faculty have provided you all the skills and tools you need to capture a husband and to staff your households with sissy maids. But to obtain maximum efficiency from male slaves you need to know about their care and feeding. So pay attention today, these are valuable lessons. Please form up outside the bus and wait for me."

The girls walked down the aisle, each one stopping to tighten their leather gloved hand into a fist and deliver a savage blow to the bus driver's right arm and shoulder. His arm was covered in black, blue and greenish bruises that never healed. Chained to his seat there was no way he could escape, even if he wanted to. But he'd accepted this for so long that although they hurt, he sat and took his beatings, offering whimpers of pain into his penis gag. The girls, for their part, delighted in seeing who could force the loudest wails from his gagged mouth.

Caroline watched this ritual with amused detachment. *At this rate he'll only be good for another year before that right arm is useless. Oh well, I'll sell him to Constance, and he can spend the rest of his days inside the stables.* Before leaving the bus she took the remote control from her pocket and pressed 'medium'. The steel balls inside the driver's butt plug began to gyrate and bounce against one another. She smiled as the driver squirmed at the anal invasion. Grabbing his wrists she brought them to his neck, locking the cuffs to his collar.

He looked at her; his eyes begging and pleading for mercy. He knew there was no relief, no mercy, never had been, never would be. But something deep inside of him still searched for what he knew he'd never find.

She saw the look, reached down and viciously pinched a nipple. *Eventually that look will be gone; he'll be destroyed, resigned to his fate. But I do like them like this, ever hopeful…right before they're completely broken.*

She left the bus and joined her fresh-faced entourage: so prim, so proper, so perfectly dressed and coifed. And so full of malevolent evil, carefully inculcated by her, "Follow me girls."

Caroline entered a code on the keypad and the sound of magnetic locks releasing could be heard behind the door as the group walked inside.

The entrance was a well appointed office area: wooden desks, fresh flowers and plants, and the usual assortment of computers and office equipment. A matronly woman with graying hair rose and embraced Caroline. "So good to see you today, and these are your girls? Here for their first milking are they? We won't disappoint them."

"Ladies," said Caroline, "this is our host and the Stable Manager, Margaret."

"Good morning girls, I'm so pleased you're with us today," Margaret said.

A chorus of "Thank you, Ma'ams" filled the office.

Margaret beamed, she always reveled in young women coming of age and taking their rightful place in the Matriarchal hierarchy. "Shall we go in girls? And if you have any questions please ask myself or any of my Warders. You may touch and handle any of our males; we keep them quite clean and hygienic, although gloves are mandatory for the actual manual milking procedures." She chuckled as she heard the usual: "cool – yech – gross – are they ticklish?" Margaret nodded to her secretary who pushed a button on her desk. With a 'whoosh' the large door slid to the side and the group stepped into the holding pens.

The girls and their escorts found themselves in the very heart of the stables. A long central corridor stretched the length of the building leading to large roll-up doors at the end. On each side of the corridor were the pens, small barred cubicles waist high. Everything was gleaming white, chrome and stainless steel. The girls squinted at the brightness.

"Yes, it is bright," said Margaret. She took sunglasses from a rack and gestured for the girls to each take a pair. She swept her arm in the direction of the pens, "They live in constant brightness, no time, no day, no night, they simply exist. They eat and they are milked." She reached into a drawer to remove a leather Tawse. "Ms. Smythe has kindly provided this beautiful Tawse as a prize for the best milker among you. It's a lovely implement that you can pass on as an heirloom to your daughters to use on their husbands." She handed it to one of the girls, "Pass it around, get a feel for it."

A Warder in a white jump suit and knee-high, spike heeled boots approached and handed Margaret a riding crop. She flexed it in her hands and turned to face the girls. "Each pen has a crop, paddle and nipple clamps to punish and discipline our stock. Use them at your pleasure. There's really no room in the pens for whips." She smiled, "I suppose that could be the single consolation to their dismal existence. Still, we can get all the results we want with these simple tools." She cut the air with a menacing slice of her crop. "Ellen," she pointed to the Warder, "will demonstrate on the first subject, and then you can each select your stock and have a go at it yourself." She turned to Caroline, "Would you like to join me for coffee while the girls learn to milk?"

"Thank you, love to."

"Girls, if I may have your attention over here." Ellen led the group to the first pen. From the wall she removed a clipboard and scanned the attached pages. "Number 723, age 53." She pointed to the man on his hands and knees on the coarse concrete floor of the pen. He was naked save for a steel collar around his neck. The collar was attached to an eyebolt anchored in the floor. It was obvious he was always on his hands and knees.

A hand shot up. "Number 723? Doesn't he have a name?"

"We give them numbers, names aren't necessary for them. Some of them haven't heard their name for years." Ellen laughed, "They may not even remember their name." She consulted the clipboard again, "If it matters, his name is, was, Donald Kremmer, sold to our stables six years ago by his wife." Number 723 never looked up at the mention of his name. She held the clipboard up so the girls could see one of the pages. "This is a Run Chart, a Statistical Process Control device. We monitor their sissy cream output to insure they produce efficiently. Although he lacked as a lover and a husband, his milking output is acceptable."

One of the girls raised her hand. "What happens when they can't produce anymore?"

"The first thing we do is check the charts and their recent history," said Ellen. "If it shows a steady and gradual decline they may be at the end of their useful life as milkers. Or it could be an aberration; maybe they're sick or off their feed. If it's something we can fix then we make the adjustment and get them back to full spunk production."

There were several giggles and murmurs at "spunk production."

Another hand shot up, "And if you can't fix the problem?"

Ellen shrugged, "They're at the end of their useful life to us. We may send them to the fields, but often they can't keep up with the physical demands of hard labor. Others end their life as furniture items, serving out their existence as ashtray holders, boot lickers. Or we sell them off, that's the most profitable in the long run, although we don't realize much revenue from even that."

"Sell them to…who?"

"Overseas markets, we don't ask what's done with them. OK girls, back to this specimen. We use standard portable milking machines, the kinds used in small operations for sheep or goats. This nipple goes over their penis and chastity device. The end of their chastity device can be removed exposing the head of the penis, which is pulled into the suction tube. Here," she motioned to one of the girls, "put your finger in there."

The girl did and Ellen turned on the machine.

"Wow," the girl said, "I can feel the suction."

"Exactly." Ellen smiled and turned off the machine. She slipped on a pair of latex gloves, squirted lube into the milking nipple, and pushed it onto his chastised penis. "We have devices to automatically massage their prostate, fucking machines if you will." She pointed to an evil looking device at the back of the pen, a large flesh-colored dildo attached to a chrome rod. "We can hook them up and walk away, come back later and collect the results." Her lips broke into an evil smile,

"But there's something about getting up close, inside and personal." She slipped two fingers inside number 723.

He gasped at the penetration, evoking laughter from the girls.

"You've done the simulators at the academy. This is really no different." Ellen gently probed and stroked while the milking machine whirred and chugged. "When you find that little bump just push on it, stroke it. Since they're in chastity, they can't get an erection, that's what makes milking so delicious for us and humiliating for them. They give up their seed, but miss that precious rush of ejaculation. Look at the tubing."

When the girls turned their attention to the clear tubing at the nipple they saw the first beads of ejaculate slowly pulsing down the tube. Ellen continued to massage the prostate.

"It looks like he's crying," said one of the girls.

Indeed, tears were streaming down the slave's face, even as he sighed with pleasure from being fondled.

"Shame, frustration and pleasure, too many emotions for him to deal with," Ellen said. "He's twice the age of you girls, but here he is, naked on his hands and knees, a virtual slave, being milked of his seed, deprived of an erection, no shred of manliness left." She bent down to whisper in his ear, "But he likes it when I put my hand up there; don't you?"

He shook and sobbed as Ellen milked the last of his seed, "Yes, yes."

"You'll note they all have nipple rings." Ellen reached under the slave to tweak his rings. The girls giggled and pointed. "You can pull on these, twist them or tweak them. There are weights on the wall that can be attached to the rings. It's fun to pummel their ass and watch their titties bounce. Some of our stock, the ones who've been here for years, have quite distended nipples. You can also use one of the chains," she pointed to the accessories on the wall, "to attach between the nipples and the retaining ring on the floor. This keeps them quite motionless, despite what you do back here." She shoved hard with her hand and number 723 lurched forward. "That won't happen when you secure the nipples."

She removed her hand, stripped off the latex gloves, removed the nipple, and stopped the machine. Ellen examined the collection container and noted the number of cc's collected, writing the number on the chart. "Not bad, he's still an acceptable producer." She extended her foot and he bent his head to kiss the toe of her boot. "They lead a bleak existence here, and are grateful for any attention they get."

A tall redhead raised her hand. "Some of them have a ring in their nose. What's that all about?"

"Discipline problems," Ellen said. "Some of them had trouble adapting to their life here. A nose ring makes it easy to lead them around and get their attention."

The girls were excited and ready to try their hand at milking a male. At Ellen's urging they dispersed throughout the stable, strolling along the pens, window shopping as they do at the mall. The hapless males could only remain on their hands and knees and cower in shame. Lady Caroline brought her girls here every semester, and the males had no choice but to submit and endure the humiliation of being milked by girls young enough to be their daughters. It was the ultimate shame and degradation, which was why Lady Caroline kept bringing her classes back.

The girls chatted endlessly as they made their selections: "I think I'll do this one." "I want this one; I've never seen balls that big; he must be full!" "Oooh, a black one, I want to do him." "Yech, this one's so fat; I'd lose my hand in there." "This one's much younger then the rest." "What do you feed them?"

Ellen circulated, answering questions and giving recommendations. "He's fat because he's relatively new. With their meager diet here they all slim down." "Yes, he's the youngest we've ever had; his mother sold him to us." "We feed them gruel, a mixture of tuna, oatmeal, water and their own cum. With a few vitamins and supplements it provides all the nutrients they need and enough calories to sustain them for their existence here."

Susan ambled along, her high-heeled court shoes clicking on the concrete floor. She deliberately stopped before a pen and looked the kneeling male in the eyes. "Hello, Daddy." Sliding back the railing, she stepped into the pen.

He didn't know how long it had been since his wife and daughter had visited the stables. There was no sense of time here: constant light, the same meals, endless monotony; it was existence, nothing more. And now she stood before him, perched on those same school-issued high heels he'd seen countless times as he'd served as a subject for some young lady's milking exercise. His body shook with an uncontrollable spasm of fear. There were never any good visits.

She sat on the stool in front of him. He heard the rustling of expensive hosiery as she crossed her silken legs. When she extended her foot his tongue automatically lapped at the sole of her shoe. It was a conditioned reflex, see a woman's shoe and lick it clean.

While his tongue worshipped her foot she opened her purse and removed her cigarettes. "Is smoking permitted here?" she asked a passing Warder.

"Of course, there's no concern about second-hand smoke with our stock. The collection equipment is self-contained and sterilized off-site." The Warder nodded to the subject. "This the one you're going to milk?"

"No, we're just having a family talk, aren't we Daddy?" Her sing-song voice didn't hide the menace in her eyes. She turned to the Warder, "Are there ashtrays?"

"Just something else to clean up," the Warder laughed, "their mouths work just as well. I'll leave you to your family reunion." The Warder walked off, slapping her crop against her leather boot.

Susan lit her cigarette and smoked in silence. "Open." She said it in a simple, everyday fashion, confident that a properly trained male would respond. And he did, tilting his head back and opening his mouth wide.

She leaned forward to blow smoke in his face and tapped an ash into the waiting mouth. A smile crossed her lips as he dutifully swallowed the ash and opened his mouth for yet another. She looked at the ring in his nose; he'd been one of the problem ones when he first arrived in the stables. "How long have you been here?" It amused her to watch his face as he tried to think. *Maybe the rumors are true; maybe they do begin to lose their cognitive abilities the longer they're here.*

"I - I don't know."

"What year is it?" She tapped more ash into his mouth.

"I, I…"

She kicked him with the toe of her high heel. "Being in here hasn't made you any smarter. Mother was right to sell you off. Our new sissy maid is much better than you." She leaned in close to whisper, "And Mother's lover, Miguel, fucks her like you never could, long and hard."

He started to cry. *Did she only come here to torment me?* "Please, please, this place, they -"

"Open." Again, the simple command shut him up and earned him more ash in his awaiting mouth. "Seven years. You've been in here over seven years. I think I was twelve when Mother finally had enough of you and sold you off."

She pulled an i-Pod from her purse and dialed up a picture. "Recognize her?" she asked.

He blinked and focused on the picture, a young girl, attractive, but not pretty. She had long blonde hair and wore a black and white maid's dress, fishnet stockings and very high heels. Most noticeable were the girl's breasts, hugely out of proportion to the rest of her.

"Yea, notice those do you?" Susan smiled and brought up another picture, a close-up of the girl's bosom. "They're 44FF's. We had to have her maid uniforms custom made to accommodate them."

He nodded, and continued to stare as she selected picture after picture: the girl in a bra and panties, the girl with bare tits showing abnormally large nipples, the girl with clothespins on her nipples, the girl sucking someone's cock, the girl being ass-fucked.

Susan shook her head with disbelief as she watched him try to think, to remember, his eyes glued to the pictures of the young girl. "Do you remember your son – my little baby step-brother?" She spoke the last words with derision.

When he looked up at her his eyes still held the same far-away, confused look.

She poked him with the i-Pod to draw his attention back to the screen. "That's your son; Violet, our assistant sissy maid is your son Robert.

He shook his head, in frustration, in denial, in confusion.

"Yes, that's right." She smiled, sat back and lit another cigarette. "Mother pegged baby brother as a loser, a wimp, early on. She knew he'd turn out like you if she didn't take matters in hand, so after she sold you off she started feminizing her step-son, Robert. Open," she flicked more ash into his mouth. "Domestic training, hormones, and of course the breast implants. Impressive aren't they? And the doctor made those hideous nipples very sensitive. I love to flick them with my fingernails, pinch them, twist them; it drives poor Violet wild. She's my personal sissy maid. Oh, she's still got a bit of manhood; Mother left that intact. But lack of use and hormones have rendered it useless except to torture her – which I do. Mother's lover, Miguel, uses Violet; that's him with his cock in her ass and her mouth. Violet loves it; she's a cock-whore. So you're in the Smythe Stables and your son is our sissy maid slut. I'd say everyone is exactly where they need to be."

She stood up, dropped her cigarette butt in his mouth, and laughed as he choked to swallow it down. "And you'll stay here; this is your life, for the rest of your life. Enjoy it Daddy." His sobs of despair didn't even cause her to look back as she spun on her heel and walked out of the pen.

Ellen stood in the center of the aisle and shouted to the girls, "Pick a specimen, we'll begin milking in a few minutes. Everyone put on the latex gloves; hygiene is mandatory, at least for *your* sake."

Susan entered the pen next to her father's. She removed the clipboard from its hook. "Number 576, age forty four, your ex-wife sent you here. What'd you do to fuck that up?" She returned the clipboard to its hook and pulled on a pair of the latex gloves, laughing at the way her subject flinched when she let the gloves snap at her wrists.

"Remove the cap on their chastity device and apply the lube to the exposed flesh." Ellen strolled up and down the aisle, ensuring her young charges were properly handling and exposing the genitals of their subjects. "More lube is better than not enough; the nipple suction will secure it once the vacuum is sufficiently established." To the giggling of the girls, and the humiliation of their subjects, Ellen offered assistance where needed. "OK, you can turn on the machines, start on the low setting and hold the nipple in place – now turn it up to medium. Can you feel it starting to hold? Let go and see if it stays." Again, Ellen helped girls here and there until everyone was ready. "All right, everyone take a place on the stool behind your subject. And don't forget about the prize of the beautiful Tawse for the one who produces the most."

The girls moved behind their subjects, the building filling with the sounds of shuffling feet and scraping of stools on the concrete,

A red-headed girl named Judy poked her head above the pens. "Hey, Susan, I got your step-dad in here. Bet I can milk him dry before you empty yours!"

"Him? He's used up, no way."

"Bet."

"Yea," Susan said. "OK, bet you that new Sissy Maid Bitch Slap DVD."

"You're on." Judy reached down and grabbed her subject's nose ring, eliciting a squeal of pain. "OK, pig face, you better put out. I want that DVD and I want to win the Tawse."

Ellen clapped her hands to get the girls' attention. "Lube up your subject and your insertion hand and start in with two fingers. When you're breaking in your own sissy husband or your domestic staff you may have to start with a single finger. But our stock has been well used and most can easily accept at least three fingers."

Number 576 quivered as Susan's gloved fingers made their way inside. No matter how many times, and it had been hundreds, he'd been violated it always evoked the same reaction.

"Like that do you?" Susan teased. She smiled as she took her free hand and stroked his nipple. It made her chuckle to watch him swoon. She leaned in to whisper in his ear, "Give me a nice big load and you'll get a treat."

He closed his eyes, lost in her seductive voice and the feel of her hair as it brushed across his shoulder. Her fingers on his nipple were soft and gentle, not punishing like some of the others. She smelled soft and fragrant, scented soap and Lilacs.

Ellen's voice rose above the chattering of the girls and the whimpering of the stock. "Push in farther and feel around for the prostate. When you find it, begin gently pushing on it. We're literally going to milk him of his seed. The suction pump simply helps to move it to the collection container once you get it out of him. Remember, if they aren't cooperating the crop and paddle are on the wall; and there are also the nipple clamps and chains."

Again 576 heard the sultry voice of his milker, "We don't need paddles or clamps do we?" Susan removed her hand from his nipple and a few seconds later held it to his mouth. "Open."

He opened his mouth and Susan dropped in a piece of chocolate. "Mmm, good isn't it? Bet you don't get anything like that. Hurry up and give me that sissy juice and you'll get another piece." As 576 sucked on his treat, Susan worked his prostate and fondled his nipple.

"You may switch the milking machines to high now," Ellen said. "Sometimes the suction at the head of the cock provides a bit of extra stimulation."

The stables reverberated with sounds of suction pumps turned to high.

Judy grabbed the paddle from the wall and delivered a stinging blow to Susan's father. Her eyes gleamed as she watched the crimson color bloom on her subject's ass. "Hurts doesn't it?" she yelled in his ear. "There's more where that came from," she struck him again. "Yea – and they'll keep coming until you deliver." She dropped the paddle to the floor and shoved her hand roughly into his ass. With her free hand she pinched his nipple while she cruelly pumped his prostate.

He whimpered at this punishing assault, tears falling from his eyes, turning the concrete floor of his pen a dark gray where they fell. *Why do they have to be so cruel?*

His tormenter was relentless, mauling his insides, crushing his nipples and screaming in his ear. "Give it up slut! Now! I don't see anything in that tube yet. You want more of the paddle, bitch?

Susan smiled at the thought of Judy's torment of her subject. *Judy's impulsive, there's more than one way to manipulate a submissive male.* She bent down to coo in her specimen's ear. "C'mon, just relax and let it a-l-l out for me. It feels good doesn't it? Hurry and get it all out and I'll give you another piece of chocolate."

576 groaned as Susan relentlessly, but gently, pumped his prostate. He felt the release as his seed slowly started to flow into the tube. *At least she's not vicious; she's not hurting me.*

"Very good, keep it up." Susan nodded as she watched the milky fluid flow down the tube. Her right hand continued to milk him, but she used her left hand to pet him, stroking his hair as one may dote on a beloved pet. "All of it baby, I want it all, relax and let it all come out."

He started to cry. It was so long since anyone had been so gentle with him, shown him any kindness.

She wiped away his tears and kissed his cheek.

"Almost done, squeeze for me, I need it all, you want to please me don't you?"

He nodded, gasping and sobbing.

Judy's screeching could be heard above the ambient noise in the stables. She had the paddle out again and was viciously spanking her subject with one hand as she shoved the other in and out. "What the fuck is wrong with you? You want more weights on those nipples? Then produce you slut!"

"Everyone, everyone," Ellen shouted. "You need to be finishing in the next few minutes. Lady Caroline will be taking you all to an afternoon tea hosted by Ms. Smythe. While you're gone we'll have submissive handlers collect and measure your milkings. The winner will be announced at the tea."

"Fuck!" Judy shouted. "Susan, your shit-for-brains step-father is fucking worthless."

Susan eased her gloved hand out of 576 and stood. She looked at Judy and smiled. "Told you, I'll expect that DVD this weekend." Before she left the pen she stepped behind her subject and delivered a vicious kick, her pointed-toe court shoe cruelly crushing 576's balls.

He shrieked with pain and lurched forward as much as his bonds would allow.

Susan grabbed his hair and pulled his head up to look him in the face. "Never take a superior female for granted slut." She spit in his face, her spittle mingling with his own tears. "We do what we want, when we want, pleasure or pain, it's our choice – ALWAYS."

"Come on girls. I'll answer any questions you have about milking on the bus ride to the Smythe mansion." Ellen gathered the girls in the aisle and they made their way out of the stable.

Another Warder ushered in a group of naked males, shuffling along in their heavy chains and manacles. The naked slaves moved into the pens, collecting the milkings, grateful that their life, though one of slavery, pain and humiliation was better than the life of those in the stables.

The girls looked out the bus windows as it made its way to the Smythe mansion. They pointed and talked as they passed groups of laborers working on the estate grounds. Verdant shrubs were trimmed into intricate shapes: rabbits, swans and even a large penis.

The the estate groundskeepers wore decidedly unconventional uniforms. Each male worker was clad in pink short-shorts and a pink crop top, both trimmed with white lace. Pink knee socks adorned their legs and their feet were shod in brown, high-heeled ankle boots. All were issued billowing straw hats held in place with a pink ribbon tied in a large bow under their chin. Their 'work gloves' were the same shocking pink.

Women overseers patroled the grounds in golf carts, inspecting the work and administering punishment and discipline for shoddy performance. The girl's found it very amusing to see a group of naked males, on their hands and knees, trimming the grass using only manicure scissors. A female guard lounged in the shade of her golf cart, enjoying a cool drink and spurring on her charges with snaps of her single-tail whip.

"Punishment detail," said Lady Caroline as they passed the naked males. "They'll spend all day trimming the grass with their tiny scissors. It's not about actually cutting the grass; there are males with push lawn mowers for that. It's about punishment."

"I don't see any riding mowers or weed whackers," said one girl. "Couldn't they get more done with power tools?"

"Certainly," Caroline said. "But Constance won't hear of it. 'Noisy infernal machines' she calls them. No, Ms. Smythe prefers a manual and more traditional approach. Rather than throw machinery and technology at a problem she uses manpower."

"You mean sissy power," said another girl.

"Exactly, that's one thing there's no shortage of, Constance has a long waiting list of applicants. When we get to the mansion be on your best behavior and remember, she is Ms. Smythe to you. When you are formally admitted into the Matriarchal Society you will then be able to address her as Constance. Feel free to ask any questions, this is to be both a fun and educational outing."

"Pony carts!" shrieked a girl from the back of the bus. Perfectly coiffed heads turned to see a meadow beyond a stand of trees. The girls could clearly make out a cart being driven around a circular track. A woman in a white blouse, white Jodhpurs and black riding boots was using her buggy whip to flick the flanks of the naked male pulling the cart.

"Yes," Caroline said, "the competitive season starts soon."

The girls assembled at the entrance and gazed with wonder at the house. Pink and gray marbled columns extending twenty-five feet in height lined the front. The circular driveway was paved with large gray stones and circled an impressive sculpted fountain of a Greek Goddess. Liveried male attendants stood aside the main entrance doors, tall and massive structures of carved wood and stained glass. The attendant's uniforms were reproductions of something from the era of the French court: tight cream-colored breeches, scarlet waist coats dripping with gold braid, black velvet shoes with large silver buckles and two-inch Louis heels, powdered wigs, long eyelashes and rouged faces. The look was more theater than functional. Although they were obviously male, the look was so androgynous that someone unfamiliar with the affairs at the Smythe mansion would obviously look twice.

"Wow, this is so totally mag," Judy said. "Ms Smythe lives fuckin' large." She looked over her shoulder to see if Lady Caroline heard her. "Sissy gardeners and fancy-ass doormen, cool."

Lady Caroline assembled her girls and started to the door. The doormen gracefully opened the doors, and with bows and flourishes ushered the giggling girls inside. Waiting for them were two elegantly dressed sissy maids who curtsied to Lady Caroline, spun on their stilettos, and minced down the long hallway.

The girl's eyes were wide as they walked passed

erotic oil paintings of women in power and authority.

"Who's that?" Sheila asked. She stood before a painting of a flaming-haired woman in a rust colored dress and blue cloak. The woman held a spear and led a group of warriors. The girls gathered around, transfixed by the sensuality and power of the work.

"It's Boudicca, leader of the Iceni, a band of Celts who staged a revolt and wreaked havoc on the Roman legions of England, sacking London and two other towns and slaughtering everyone she and her hordes could find." Amy pushed her glasses up on her nose. Of course she would have that information at her disposal. She was in her final year, rather plain in looks, but gifted with an extremely high IQ. And she possessed a facility with a single tail whip that impressed even her instructors. Yet it was her cold intellect and seeming lack of emotion that struck fear into the male practice subjects. The prettier girls certainly aroused and excited them, but it was Amy who made them wet themselves during a pre-discipline inspection.

Lady Caroline nodded with approval. She found something to love about all her girls, with Amy it was intellect and cruelty. "She's quite right; Boudicca was a fearsome warrior; there is a statue of her in London. I believe that the gift shop at the Stables has prints of this work; you may want to check that out when we go back this afternoon." She pointed across the hall to another painting. "This is the painting of Omphale, the Queen who bought Hercules as a slave. Hercules served her for three years. Some legends say that he was humiliated by wearing women's clothes and doing traditional feminine tasks. Female domination, power and authority have a rich history both in legend," she pointed to the Hercules paining, "and in fact," as she turned and pointed to the painting of Boudicca.

"It's beautiful," Sheila said, "the way that the painter draws the eye to Omphale in the center, with the man kneeling before her." She turned Lady Caroline, "Is it real?"

Lady Caroline allowed a thin smile to cross her lips. She'd assisted Constance in the acquisition of this work and knew that the one in the Getty Museum – *that* one was a fake. "It's very valuable – come girls, there's more to see." She waved her hand, indicating to the two sissy maids to continue to lead the way to the salon.

Further down the hall they encountered the alcoves; tall enough to house a person – which they did. Each alcove held a naked, or erotically clothed male, all in suggestive poses. They stood, pale and motionless.

"Look, statues of slaves," Jennifer said. "Sweet, I bet they cost a lot, they look so – EEEK! It's eyes moved – no, no shit, they're alive."

"Girls," Lady Caroline took control. "Yes, they're living statues. Something new that Smythe Enterprises is developing. These are prototypes; you're among the first to see them. Come here."

The girls gathered around.

"They are living and breathing males," Caroline explained. "They've been denuded of all body hair and their skin has been bleached, or in some cases tinted, depending on their specific use as a statue. A marbled body tint is still in development. For now an alabaster-toned bleaching seems to work best."

"Can they hear us?"

"Certainly, their brains are fully functioning, or as functioning as one can expect from a male brain." This brought general laughter from the girls. "They can see and hear us, but can't move, their muscular functions are paralyzed."

There was a chorus of, "how?"

"It's a derivative of Curare from South America, something that was tweaked by the scientists in Smythe Laboratories. It paralyzes the subject, greatly slows down the metabolic system, but leaves the senses fully intact – that was the difficult part – paralyze movement, but leave them able to feel, everything. They're on display for twelve hours and then taken back to maintenance where they are hydrated, fed intravenously, and given enemas. Tomorrow morning will find them back on display."

Caroline removed a small leather Quirt from her purse. "Watch the eyes, not me, keep watching his eyes."

The girls intently stared at the man's eyes.

Caroline lightly slapped the statue's penis. "You know what's coming don't you? Your cock is going to be cruelly whipped as an object lesson to a group of young ladies. It's going to be painful, but you can't run, can't even move." She continued to lightly slap at the penis, teasing it and the appendage attached to it. "You're going to be punished, suffer horribly and there's nothing you can do. It's inevitable, your situation is hopeless. Pain – you are going to feel pain."

"I see it."

"Yes, me too."

"Yea, his eyes, everything about him is frozen but I can see the fear building in his eyes."

"Excellent girls, watch…" Caroline delivered two stinging blows that made the sissy maid attendants wince and pull their legs together. They'd witnessed this too many times. No matter what the pain and humiliation of being a sissy maid, it was better than being a statue slave. Caroline struck again, a blow that would have brought a man screaming to his knees, but the living statue remained motionless, save for the tears falling from his eyes.

"Oh yea, it's in his eyes, first fear, and now pain."

"You could see his emotions change, just in his eyes, nothing else."

"It's a valuable lesson girls," Caroline returned the Quirt to her purse. "Submissives are liable to say anything, especially in a moment of pain or excitement. Pay more attention to how they say something, rather than what they say. And watch their body language, often the body will tell you what they can't or won't say. But above all, watch their eyes."

"Wow, that's some drug, bet the person who came up with that is gonna be rich" Judy said.

Caroline smiled, "You'd lose that bet. The inventor, a Smythe Labs chemist, tried to sell it off to another company, a bit of industrial espionage."

"What happened to him?"

"Was he arrested?"

"No girls, Constance handles these things internally. He's right over there." Caroline pointed to the figure in the alcove across the hall.

The girls moved over en masse to view the figure precariously balanced on eight-inch heeled ballet boots.

"Wow, that's gotta hurt."

"I like high heels, but that…"

"He must love to get them off at the end of the day."

"Actually not, Constance had the bones in his feet crushed and then fused into the extreme ballet position by a team of doctors who do – special projects – for her." Caroline ran a hand over the shiny patent ballet boot. "No, I'm afraid the only option for this one is to go through life continually on tip toes. Come girls, Constance is expecting us."

Judy sidled up to Susan, "That slave in the ballet boots, it's sort of like safe sex."

"Safe sex?" Susan asked. "I don't get it."

"Don't fuck with Ms Pennington Smythe."

Lady Caroline led her charges down the hall, stopping occasionally to observe and comment on other living statues. The girls poked, prodded, slapped and pinched the statue slaves, laughing at the terrified responses in the prisoner's eyes.

The two sissy maids slowed as they neared the end of the hallway, turned and curtsied. They waited until Lady Caroline led the last girl into the lounge, then the maids curtsied again and minced back down the hall to take up their stations at the entrance.

The girls found themselves in the richly, well-appointed lounge. One entire wall was windows and French Doors, the afternoon light only slightly diffused by elegant and expensive sheers. The doors opened onto a veranda, beyond which was the Arboretum where the girls saw naked males working. The other walls were finished in expensive wallpaper and exotic wood wainscoting. Erotic paintings and tapestries of women dominating men hung from the walls.

Sissy maids scurried about the room; their only sounds the clicking of their heels on the intricate parquet wood floor and the rustling of their petticoats. They were putting the last touches to tables adorned with crisp white linen, gleaming silver flatware and polished china and crystal.

Judy grabbed Susan's sleeve and pulled her around to face the door. "That's her...it's her."

Susan slapped at Judy's hand, "Don't point, it's not polite." But she followed the track of Judy's finger to the woman who dominated the doorway. Susan's eyes alighted on a tall woman, or at least she looked tall in her expensive designer platforms; they easily added six inches to her height. When the woman turned to greet a friend Susan saw the seams of her expensive stockings.

"It's her, Ms Smythe," Judy whispered.

"Yea…" Susan said. She continued to watch as their host made her way into the room. Susan took note of their hosts's elegant couture, an exquisitely cut Chanel suit and. Strings of pearls encircled her neck and bracelets of pearls, gold and precious stones stood out against the long black leather gloves that disappeared into the three quarter length sleeves of her jacket.

"Look, look," Judy pulled on Susan's sleeve and pointed again. "She's got a slave on a leash."

"Yes – a slave," Lady Caroline gracefully moved to her two young charges, "and also her husband."

The three of them watched as Ms Smythe pulled her crawling slave into the room. She moved about the room, never watching the crawling creature behind her, confident that it would follow and obey any and all commands of the leash and hands.

"Wow, that rocks, she's awesome," Judy said.

"Do control yourself," Caroline admonished.

Constance approached her friend and the two embraced, "Caroline, lovely for you to visit," she cast a smile at Susan and Judy, "and to bring your girls." She turned to the girls, "Did you enjoy your morning at the stables."

"Oh, yes," Susan said. "Practice on the classroom simulators in the lab is one thing, but a real live male, it really makes a difference."

A slight twitch of the leash brought the crawling husband to heel and Constance reached out with her black gloved hand to pet his head. "Milking your future husband, and any of your sissy maid servant staff, is an important ritual. It reinforces their submission, and if your lover is there to watch, it makes it even more humiliating."

"Having your lover actually doing the milking can be even more humiliating," Caroline added.

A uniformed sissy maid minced up and curtsied before Constance, "Everything is ready, Madam."

Constance merely nodded and the sissy maid curtsied and teetered away on a pair of impossibly high stilettos.

A second hand gesture brought the naked husband back to his hands and knees as Constance ushered the group forward with a wave of her hand, "Let's be seated, shall we?"

Lady Caroline rose from her seat at the head table and the room stilled. "I want to thank our hostess for making her wonderful stables and staff available to us this morning."

Polite applause rippled throughout the room as Constance smiled and nodded.

"The lessons you learned today," Caroline continued, "will serve you well as the matriarchal leaders you will become. Males will submit to you, both willingly and unwillingly, and I have every confidence that you will rise to each occasion, establish your dominance and ensure the continuation of female supremacy."

Caroline turned and motioned to a uniformed sissy maid who stepped forward, holding a silver tray. "Today, one of you distinguished yourself by your most excellent performance in the stables. The prize, the beautiful leather Tawse from Ms Smythe, goes to Gretchen Covington."

A giddy group at a middle table high-fived as Gretchen stood and walked to the head table. She received her prize from Constance and strutted back to her table, flicking the Tawse as she went. At the table the girls took turns passing around the Tawse, and their sissy maid attendant, whose backside was reddened and welted by repeated applications of the wicked leather tool.

The afternoon reception continued, with the girls drinking tea and eating sandwiches and pastries, all served by a bevy of submissive sissy maids. Each table had two maids in attendance, and it wasn't nearly enough to serve the six demanding young Mistresses who delighted in ordering the maids about, slapping, pinching and kicking them. Caroline escorted Constance from table to table, introducing her to the girls in her class.

"OK," Judy pouted, "so neither of us won the prize."

Susan tightened her grip on a sissy maid's nipple and shook her head as the sissy gasped. "Yea, still, it's been a good day. I mean – to see all those males, in the stables, kneeling, day after day – and the way Ms Smythe lives. Wow."

"Yea," Judy grabbed the sissy maid's other nipple and squeezed, "and..."

"And," Susan pinched the nipple harder and smiled as she watched the sissy's knees wobble, "and this is what I want." She swept her free hand to the room.

"We graduate in two months," Judy said.

"Then we find husbands," Susan ground the nipple between her fingers.

"And lovers," smiled Judy, as she likewise tortured the sissy's nipple.

"And sissy maids," they said in unison as their demon grips on the sissy's nipples drove him to his knees.

END ?

About the Author

Constance Pennington Smythe

Constance Pennington Smythe is an erotic author. She is retired from the corporate world, has lived abroad, and possesses multiple degrees.

www.cpsmythe.com

Gwendolyn's Revenge

Sardax graciously provided one of his favorite illustrations. Hmmm, dear reader, who do you wish *you* could be in this picture?

About the Illustrator

Sardax

Sardax is an English artist living in London who has worked in the specific field of "femdom illustration " for over 20 years.

He started drawing in his student years mainly for his own pleasure then contributed to various magazines such as Skin Two, Shiny and Leg Show, and books covering the disciplinary field. In 2006, The Art of Sardax was published by The Erotic Print Society. By early 2007 it had sold out worldwide.

From his studio he lives quietly dividing his time between personal commissions for dominas and lifestyle couples, maintaining and updating his own website and occasionally producing illustrations and graphics for other websites when time allows. He listens to classical music and has a flair for languages.

More information can be found on his website:

www.sardax.com

Mistress Karin

Constance Pennington Smythe

What happens when a man gets his wish to be submisisve? What happens when a woman embraces her dominant self? For Karin Calloway and her hapless husband, otherwise known as her maid Suzette, it becomes an erotic power exchange that gives them both what they desire. Is Suzette destined to become a cuckolded sissy maid? What new humiliations and torments will Karin and her evil friends, Trudi the German dance instructor and socialite Sheila Remington, visit on poor Suzette?

ISBN 978-1-934446-11-9

Enjoy an excerpt from:

Mistress Karin

By

Constance Pennington Smythe

*K*arin used a small piece of toast to wipe up the egg yolk on her breakfast plate. Without looking, she held out the morsel of food and felt it gently removed from her hand. She didn't have to see the scene unfold to know what happened. These small offerings had become valued treats for Suzette.

On some mornings Karin snapped her fingers and pointed to the floor. Suzette immediately knelt beside her Mistress, hoping that her bland diet might be augmented by those few precious scraps of 'real' food. Since her submission her diet had been meager at best. The morning gruel, often flavored with cigarette ashes, Mistress's 'nectar' or spit was supplanted by a wretched concoction called *Prison Loaf*. Karin discovered the loaf during a web search and it now formed the basis of Suzette's second meal of the day. The loaf was a mixture of grated carrots, wheat bread, artificial cheese, spinach, beans, and raisins – among other items. It was unappetizing, and purposely meant to be. That's why Suzette would literally sit and beg for table scraps.

Karin idly turned the business pages and sipped her coffee. "How long since you've been to the office?"

"Maybe two months, Mistress?" He phrased it as a question, he truly didn't know.

She didn't press the issue, content with his answer. It was what she wanted – his isolation from the world at large – total focus and dependence on her. He was kept busy all day with chores, tasks, dance lessons, aerobic workouts in cute pink leotards. He was denied computer and television access, she'd locked those out. Newspapers were forbidden to him, but he was allowed women's magazines: *Vogue*, *Good Housekeeping,* and *Glamour*.

"Three months," she said. "It's been three months since you had your –'breakdown' – and had to take time off from work. But I've been able to fill in nicely for you; after all, Daddy did leave the company to me."

"Yes, Mistress, but I thought –"

"Wrong! You thought wrong, and that's why I'm doing the thinking now. You thought that the executive with the perfect wife was the ideal. And I agree with you." She waited, wondering if that statement meant he would think they were going back to the old way; he as the CEO and she as the trophy wife. A slight smile crossed her lips as she watched his eyes light up with that hoped-for realization. She'd grown to love these moments, watching as he rose to the bait and savoring his utter desolation when she pulled out the rug and crushed his hopes. *If only his hopes were some kind of living, organic thing that I could crush with my stiletto, feel the spike heel puncture it, watch the life force slowly drain away.*

"One of the girls from the office will be coming by today." She looked him in the eyes; she wanted to remember this moment – and his reaction. "They'll be bringing papers for you to sign, your resignation."

He started to talk, even though he knew he didn't have permission. When Karin held up her hand he quickly shut his mouth.

"You will resign from your position as CEO. You will sign over all of your shares and interests in the company to me. Furthermore, you will sign over all other assets, financial and material, to me." The shock on his face, the fear, it was priceless. "You will sign a general power of attorney giving me complete control over you.

"Yes, we are going to have the perfect corporate marriage. I'm going to be the powerful, high-priced executive. And you, you my little slut, will be the trophy wife, or, in your case, the trophy sissy maid husband. As the executive I'll have trophy lovers, and you will serve them as you do me."

His shoulders fell and his chin dropped to his chest. Karin was surprised at how easily he yielded his manhood to her. She'd now taken everything, reduced him to a servant in her house. "You will sign all the papers put before you."

He meekly nodded, "Yes, Mistress."

She held out a piece of bacon and watched as his eyes lit up and he gently took it between his lips. *I destroy his career, his marriage; take his freedom and his manhood, and a scrap of bacon makes it all better.*

Karin visualized her basement project: the cage, computer, restraints and accessories. Her experiments with operant conditioning and behavior modification worked with Steven; maybe she was on to something.

She rose from the table and walked to the foyer, her husband crawling obediently at her side. "You have your list of chores. And spend thirty minutes practicing walking with the book on your head. Wear your five inch heels; work on that posture and taking the short and dainty steps. There will be times when you won't be crouching and short so you're looking up to women. I may want to pimp you out as a tranny, fetish runway model." She laughed at the thought; Steven, now Suzette, in stilettos, strutting the catwalk and shaking his submissive ass to the gathered throng.

"Be sure to sign all the papers this afternoon. I want this over, behind us, so we can move on. There's no going back." She looked down to see her husband on his knees, planting loving kisses on the toes of her stylish high heels. *No arguments, he simply accepts his situation...amazing. What started out as sex games, a little B & D...* "You'll still be my husband; you'll still keep your cock and balls, although that cock will seldom be out of chastity. And when it is, I can guarantee you won't enjoy it and you'll beg to lock it up. I don't want you to ever forget what you were...or how far you've fallen." She reached down and patted him on the head. "This really is best, for both of us."

His eyes met hers; he nodded his agreement and returned his lips to her shoes.

What can be better than a Mistress and her submissive male? How about two Mistresses and their submissive males - and their Alpha Male friends? What happens when Karin meets and mentors Joanna? It surely can't be good for their hapless maids, Suzette and Donna. Fun will be had by all, or maybe not. Follow the further adventures of Dominant Women and their submissive males in: The Breaking Cage

ISBN 978-1-934446-25-6

Enjoy an excerpt from:

The Breaking Cage

Constance Pennington Smythe

Karin Calloway relaxed in her chair
and absently turned the pages of a magazine as the
warm water and heated stones in the footbath soaked
away the stresses of her day. Scents of vanilla and
lavender filled the air; sconces on the wall gave the
room a muted amber glow. The New Age music in the
background, harps and flutes, that was something she
could do without. Some vintage Sinatra, Old Blue Eyes
with the Nelson Riddle Orchestra, or maybe even some
Harry Connick Jr. would be more to her liking; elegant
and classy as herself.

She watched a petite spa technician in a too-tight,
too-short white dress administer a pedicure to another
customer. She'd noted the girl's name badge, Tammy,
when she'd started the footbath. Karin's eyes couldn't
help but linger on the taut fabric as it stretched over
those young, firm hips. *VPL, a fashion no-no, but there's
something about her.*

The woman receiving Tammy's attentions was close to Karin's age and quite striking. Their eyes met when Karin entered the room and they exchanged polite smiles and nods in silent greeting. Then they both went back to their magazines and moments of selfish indulgence and pampering.

"Almost finished, Ma'am, your feet didn't need that much work. You're very fortunate to have a husband who takes care of them," Tammy said.

Karin raised her eyes and glanced over the top of her magazine, intrigued by the conversation.

Tammy turned to Karin. "I'll be right with you Ms. Calloway." She gathered up her things and prepared to move to Karin when the other woman spoke.

"Tammy!"

Tammy turned to face her client, who silently pointed to her feet.

Karin dropped the magazine, her terrycloth robe enfolding the pages. Something was going to happen and she didn't want to miss it.

Tammy stepped before her customer, knelt and reverently placed a tender kiss on the top of each foot. She released the feet and looked up to see the woman smiling down at her, but silently demanding more. Tammy picked up the pan of water from the footbath, brought it to her lips and took a drink, her pink tongue licking the residue from her lips. The woman in the chair nodded approvingly. The ritual act of obeisance completed, Tammy rose, set the pan on a shelf and gathered her things. She cast an embarrassed look at Karin, "I'll be right with you Ms. Calloway."

Karin's eyes followed Tammy as she left, then she

turned her gaze to the woman across the room.

The woman rose, tightened her robe, and walked to Karin. "I hope I didn't shock you".

Karin smiled and shrugged her shoulders, "actually, not at all."

"Really? Some would be shocked at such an overt and submissive display."

Karin's green eyes narrowed and she pursed her lips as if to consider. "Some would, ones who don't understand the desperate needs and nature of those who would be submissive. She said your husband does your feet?"

"Yes, quite well in fact. But I also enjoy the pampering here. And," she said, casting her eyes to the door, "Tammy is such a treasure."

"I quite agree, she is - special," Karin said, extending a hand. "My name is Karin Calloway."

"Joanna, Joanna Barnes," said the other woman, taking Karin's hand and smiling. "We really must get together."

Joanna added cream to her coffee. "I've not seen you at the spa before."

Karin dabbed at her lips with a napkin and returned it to the table. "Yes, I usually go to Giovanni's, but they're remodeling. Based on the performance of your lovely little Tammy I may consider switching locations. You noticed her submissive nature right off?"

"Not immediately, but even at the first appointment there was definitely something about the way she touched my feet, almost a - reverence."

Karin nodded. "Not surprising, someone with a strong submissive need couldn't help but exhibit some of that on the job, kneeling, giving pedicures, serving and waiting. She probably chose that vocation specifically for those reasons. How far have you taken her?"

"Only what you witnessed, foot kissing and drinking my footbath."

"Still, it makes for a wonderfully entertaining afternoon."

"Most entertaining."

Karin leaned back and considered her next question. "You said your husband does your feet. Is he submissive?"

"He likes to be dominated." Joanna paused, unsure how much to reveal to her new-found friend. "Get tied up and spanked. It was a bit of a shock at first, but as I got more comfortable with it I began to see it in more places. I saw the same look in Tammy's eyes that I'd seen in my husband's and out of curiosity I pushed it to see how far she'd go. I enjoy it: the power of having someone submit to me."

"How far have you gone with your husband?"

"Some bondage, foot kissing, he's bought crops, whips and paddles that I use on him."

"Uh-huh, sounds typical." Karin studied Joanna for a moment and leaned forward; here was new blood, a potential convert to the sisterhood. "How far would you like it to go?"

Joanna shrugged, having never considered the question. "I don't know. How far is there - to go, I mean?"

Karin's lips curled into a demonic smile, time to seal another submissive's fate. "All the way, complete submission to you, 24/7, or whenever you desire, complete service, absolute obedience. Admittedly it's not for everyone, but there can be some advantages - for you."

"I'm not sure." Joanna drummed her nails on the table nervously. "I can't imagine what that would be like. Even if it's something that I wanted – I mean; would Gary want to go that far?"

"That's your first mistake..." Karin settled back in her chair allowing Joanna some space. "...allowing him a choice in the matter."

Joanna hesitated. "I don't know, up until now it's been..."

"Would you like to see how it can be, how far it can go?"

Joanna silently nodded.

"Come see me on Friday...alone."

COMING SOON

The third book in the Karin series: The circle of Dominant Women grows as Joanna introduces her friend Simone to the advantages of chastised, submissive, sissy maids. Joanna invites friend Simone and her husband Scott for the weekend, where Gary is outed as sissy maid Donna, and spends the weekend as a sex toy.

Weekend With Friends

by

Constance Pennington Smythe

"He really does anything you say?" Simone asked incredulously.

Joanna nodded and smiled, slowly drawing out her reply, "Anything."

The two friends and work colleagues were enjoying a glass of wine on a Friday evening. As they drank they discussed men and relationships, the talk becoming bawdier as the grape was consumed: *in vino veritas.*

"Yes, he's been my total submissive for quite some time now. I am the Goddess and he is my slave. I am a woman of total leisure and supreme head of the house." Joanna made the statement matter-of-factly.

Simone took another sip of wine and placed her

glass on the table. "Damn, no wonder your house is so clean and you have all this free time. You make him do everything?"

"Actually I really don't have to 'make' him do much at all. At this point, he's so pussy-whipped I only 'make' him do things to see him squirm. But it is fun to try to find new ways to push his buttons."

"What about sex?" Simone asked.

"Hell, I get as much as I want, when I want it, the way I want it, although it's almost never penetrative sex, at least from him. No, I'm afraid his little 'thing' has pretty much been reduced to an implement of torment and frustration for him."

Simone shook her head in amazement.

"I've got his little wanker under lock and key," Joanna continued. "I really don't need it and he can't get to it."

"You don't!" Simone said.

Joanna smiled, reached into her purse and fished out a small key on a golden chain. She held it out to Simone. "If I dangled this in front of Gary he'd be down on his knees in a second, waiting to do whatever I demand."

Simone shook her head in disbelief and drank the rest of her wine. "Really?"

Joanna nodded, "Really."

Simone cautiously eyed Joanna and leaned in closer. "So, uh, what kinds of things do you, uh, do - exactly."

Joanna laughed. "Shit, Simone. Don't you ever cruise stuff on the web, read Variations, Penthouse Letters, play little sex games?"

Simone shifted nervously in her chair. "Well, yea, I mean, Scott and I have seen some videos and sometimes he buys these magazines and, and - I mean damn, Joanna; you're talking the real shit, right?"

Joanna narrowed her eyes over the top of her wine glass and deliberately nodded at her friend.

Simone sat back in her chair and sighed. *What's this all about? Where is this all going?* Another question obviously on her mind, she studied Joanna. "So, are you like, a, a Dominatrix?"

Joanna reached into her purse for a silver cigarette case and languidly placed a cigarillo in a holder. "If you're asking me if I dress up in leather and high-heeled boots and carry a whip and a riding crop, yes. If you're asking me if I put Gary in bondage and beat him, yes. If you're asking if I fuck him in the ass with a strap-on and put nipple clamps on him, yes."

Simone stared, wide-eyed.

Joanna took a drag from her cigarette and expelled a sensuous stream of smoke. "The idea excites you, doesn't it?"

Simone leaned back as if trying to maintain some space from Joanna. "Well, I mean, yeah. I never really knew any body that actually did that kind of stuff, or at least admitted to it."

Joanna reclined in her chair and studied her friend. There was a moment of awkward silence while Simone played with her wine glass and Joanna finished her cigarillo.

Joanna leaned forward and purred, "Would you like to see it? Would you like to watch Gary submit to us, to crawl and kiss our feet?"

Simone felt the wetness in her sex; the idea did excite her. Hell, Scott read his damned porno mags and sometimes they rented 'fuck-me-suck-me' videos, but sex didn't seem to be as exciting these last few years. Yet, here was her friend Joanna, a good ten years older, and having a great sex life; a life that Simone could not imagine. *Yea, why not* she thought, *what's the harm in just checking it out?* Simone tried to be nonchalant, "Sure, I'd like that sometime."

Joanna cocked her head, "Now?" she asked.

Simone lost her composed façade. "What, you mean now? Tonight?"

Joanna shrugged her shoulders in a 'why not' gesture.

Simone felt warm. Was it the wine or the steamy topic of conversation? The kids were out doing some Friday night activity and Scott was off doing who knows what. She was out with Joanna because she had the early part of the evening free, so why not? She regained her composure enough to say, "Yes, Joanna, I'd be very interested to see what you are up to. You surprise me, you really do surprise me."

Joanna reached across the table, smiled and reassuringly took Simone's hand. "You won't regret this. It will be fun." She signaled the cute young waiter for the check.

Dear Readers,

I'm working on stories for Volume II of a short story collection. Here's a little tidbit of things to come. Do enjoy,

Constance Pennington Smythe

"Depth and endurance, Darling," Corrine Belgarde sipped her coffee from a bone china cup. She glanced at her husband, who struggled with the cock that was filling his mouth. "You're fighting it, and you're not even halfway there."

Her attention was drawn to her Blackberry. She placed her coffee on the matching china saucer and picked up her electronic lifeline. Her elegant hands and beautifully manicured nails tapped at keys and scrolled to the newest message. *Damn it, Karl! I need those charts before the two o'clock meeting!*

She checked her husband's feet; his heels were nearly touching the floor. She picked up a leather riding crop and struck him three times on his naked thigh. "Tippy toes, sweetheart. Up!"

He immediately rose higher on his toes, as the red welts rose on his skin.

Corrine crossed her legs and sat back on the stool at the breakfast bar. She took a moment to study her husband. He was naked, save for the small, dainty, white lace apron. It was tied in the back with a large frilly bow and the small front did nothing to hide his nakedness. Not that there was much to see; his cock was safely ensconced in a chastity device, a CB-3000. He stood on his tiptoes, bent at the waist, with his hands clasped demurely behind his back. His mouth was hovered over a realistic phallus, attached to the breakfast bar by its suction cup base.

"Half-hearted efforts simply will not do," Corrine said. "Remember when you used to watch football? Sit on that fat ass and watch TV? Before you confessed those secret sissy desires?" She saw that look in his eyes as he tried to remember a life before submission, before pain and humiliation. She patted his head, "Don't strain yourself, baby, that was a different you. But you still have a position on *my* team. You're a wide receiver, you go long and deep." She smiled, pleased with her little joke. She poked his ass with her crop, "And you're my tight end, it's your job to get open."

The crop lashed out again, a stinging blow that made him wince and issue a muffled squeal past his cock filled lips.

"Tip Toes! Up!" Corrine lovingly stroked the crop over his back; the continual mix of pain and pleasure, love and scorn, kept his psyche continually off balance. "I realize your feet and legs hurt," she cooed, "but this is training, conditioning. If you can do it with no support, think how easier and effortless it will seem with shoes, even if they are five or six inch spike heels."

He mumbled an unintelligible reply past the cock in his mouth.

"I'll take that as agreement. Now, I want you to back off that cock and get up as high as you can on those tip toes." She watched as her husband lifted his mouth from the cock and struggled to raise himself higher on his toes. His feet and legs were obviously screaming sheets of pain. But to disobey? That would invite something infinitely worse.

Corrine studied the object of his torment. Its glossy surface now glistened with his saliva. It bobbed hideously from the suction cup base that held it fast to the expensive granite breakfast bar. As cocks went she supposed it was average sized, *perhaps a bit larger than average? Certainly larger than his, one of the reasons that quite useless tool is now locked away.* Corrine had discovered the joy of real cocks, and she was committed to ensuring that her sissy hubby also learned of their joy, in his own manner. The object of his affection this day was six inches long from the realistic balls to its bulbous end. It measured nearly five inches in circumference; certainly a mouthful this morning. *But he'll learn to take all manner of cocks, that's what this is about, that's his fate.*

She poured herself more coffee, taking her time, noting how his legs began to quiver. *Poor thing must be in agony.* "Some men," she began her lecture, "are simply going to pull you down on them, fuck that pretty little face of yours. Others might relax and let *you* do the work, woo and seduce their cock." She smiled at the image of her husband on his knees, with Rick's magnificent cock filling his mouth. She looked at her watch; there was time for one more lesson. "I want you to go down on the cock, slowly walk down its length with your lips. All the way, darling; I want to see a lipstick imprint on those balls. Relax, breathe, and keep your eyes open."

He took a deep breath, opened his lips and took the head of the cock into his mouth. He slowly worked his way down, feeling the cock penetrate further and stretch his mouth wider. Her imagination seemed cruel and endless; he was precariously positioned on his toes and his mouth, a balancing act of discomfort and humiliation. The further the cock penetrated the more he fought the urge to gag.

"Not bad," she commented, "almost there. Granted it's not as big as Rick's cock, but you've got to begin somewhere. All the way down, I want that lower lip to caress those balls."

He felt her hand on the back of his head, pushing him down those last few precious millimeters.

"Stay," she whispered. "Feels good doesn't it? To have your mouth filled with a cock? Think how nice it will be with a real one, one that's warm, with blood pulsing through the veins, sweet pre-cum on your tongue." Her hand caressed his check, "Relax and breathe."

Slowly she pulled him off, nodding with approval at the lipstick mark on the balls and the stream of saliva that hung from his tongue to the wet, slimy cock. "Very nice, now lick it clean, always be ready to clean a cock that's been used." Again she imagined Rick's cock, fresh from her dripping sex, and her hubby on his knees, licking clean the cock that had so recently pleasured her.

"Get your lines book," she ordered.

Corrine watched her submissive husband tip toe down the hall to his 'maid's bedroom. "Higher on those toes!" she commanded, "hands on hips." A smile crossed her lips as he sashayed down the hall, his hands on his hips and his exaggerated walk giving him a sexy sway. *Yes, you're going to be the perfect party toy, my own cock sucking slut.*

He returned the same way, balancing on his tip toes, his left hand placed sexily on his hip, and his right hand daintily holding his pink 'lines' book. He stopped before his wife and executed the best curtsey he could, while remaining perched on his toes.

Corrine barely noticed him and didn't acknowledge the curtsey, although she knew he'd perform one; he'd been trained to do so. She slid her Blackberry back in its case and dropped it in her purse. "Write this down, 'Sissy wants a great big cock in her mouth'.

Her sissy hubby carefully wrote the humiliating passage, using a pen with purple ink on the pink pages of the notebook.

"Write that today," Corrine said, "fill a page with that line. No wait, do two, no, go ahead and do four, yes four pages. And I want you to practice on this cock today, do ten minutes of cock sucking, every hour, on the hour. Practice all the things you've been working on: kissing the head, licking the shaft, taking it deep, sucking the balls."

She reached out with her right hand and stroked his nipple. She pinched it, rolled it between her fingers. She smiled as he swooned and went weak in his knees. *Such a slut!* She pulled upwards, "Up, higher, pretend you're wearing six inch stilettos."

He struggled upwards on shaking legs. His feet and calves were screaming sheets of pain. He knew that sometime during the day or night they'd cramp up into tight balls of agony.

She tightened her grip on the nipple and pulled him even higher. "Dress after I leave: maid uniform, stockings, heels. Practice your sexy walk as you move about the house doing your chores. Change your shoes throughout the day; it's critical you're able to walk sexily in all of them. But stay on your feet! No sitting."

She released the grip on his nipple, "Do you want me to trample your hands?"

"P-p-please, Mistress."

She snapped her fingers and he assumed a position on his hands and knees. His hands were flat on the cold, hard tile floor of the kitchen. The tips of his fingers lay before the pointed toes of her wicked stilettos.

He watched as her right shoe lifted from the floor and poised over his left hand. When the leather sole kissed the top of his hand he took a breath.

She rose, placing all her weight on the ball of her foot. "See the advantages of balance? Not that you'd ever be in any different position then you are, on your knees, your hand beneath my foot." Her foot slowly twisted. "Mmmm, feels good doesn't it?"

Recommended Reading

There many books on the topics of Female Domination, BDSM, Cross-Dressing and other aspects of the alternative lifestyle. The following are a few from the current canon on the subjects and are recommended reading for a woman who wants to learn more about this lifestyle. This list is by no means complete, but these are works with which I have personal familiarity.

Female Domination

Female Domination: An exploration of the male desire for Loving Female Authority © 2003 by Elise Sutton

The Art of Sensual Female DOMINANCE: A guide for Women © 1998 by Claudia Varrin

The Sexually Dominant Woman: A Workbook for Nervous Beginners © 1998 by Lady Green

The Mistress Manual: The Good Girl's Guide to Female Dominance © 2000 by Mistress Lorelei

The Training and Education of a Husband Vol. I © 1996 by Patricia de Gifford

The Training and Education of a Husband Vol. II © 1996 by Patricia de Gifford

Sex Tips from a Dominatrix © 1999 by Patricia Payne

Sissy Maids

A Charm School for Sissy Maids © 2001 by Mistress Lorelei

Training With Miss Abernathy: A Workbook for Erotic Slaves and their Owners © 1998 by Christina Abernathy

Miss Abernathy's Concise Slave Training Manual © 1996 by Christina Abernathy

Cross-Dressing

Miss Vera's Finishing School for **Boys** *Who Want to be* **Girls** © 1997 by Veronica Vera

Miss Vera's Cross-Dress for Success © 2002 by Veronica Vera

BDSM

Screw the Roses, Send Me the Thorns: The Romance and Sexual Sorcery of Sadomasochism © 1995 by Philip Miller and Molly Devon

Learning the Ropes: A Basic Guide to Safe and Fun S/M Lovemaking © 1992 by Race Bannon

Recommended Web Sites

Don't forget the search capabilities of the world-wide-web.

<u>Female Domination</u>

www.elisesutton-homestead.com

www.akashaweb.com

www.femdomdestiny.com

<u>Cross-Dressing</u>

www.crossdresslasvegas.com

www.glamourboutique.com

www.pierresilber.com

www.xdress.com

<u>Chastity</u>

www.keptforher.com

www.cb-2000.com

www.tpe.com (Chastity info via the Altarboy link)

www.chastitylifestyle.com

www.chastitymansion.com

Chatting
with
Constance Pennington Smythe

I actually correspond with my fans and readers. Here are excerpts from various IM dialogues with some of my favorite 'gurls'.

Note 1: These correspondences have been edited to delete any personal identities, but otherwise reflect the actual dialogues between me and my on-line *gurls*.

Note 2: 'petal' is my own in-house submissive.

lilly: Good evening Mistress<curtsey>

Constance Pennington Smythe: Hello, baby. I just got back from supper, at a lovely place downtown. And how are you?

lilly: I am better than wonderful; I'm all alone! and feeling like a complete sissy

Constance Pennington Smythe: And are you properly dressed' to be talking with me? Hmmm?

lilly: Why yes Ma'am i do hope so although I'm only in my bra and panties and a robe

Constance Pennington Smythe: Do you smell pretty for me? Why not add a spritz of something feminine for me, OK?

lilly: okay 1 minute please Ma'am, brb

lilly: I'm back Ma'am i smell like a little sissy flower

Constance Pennington Smythe: Lovely. Give the nipples a little pinch to get some color in them, make them nice and rosy - and then we can talk.

lilly: Yes Ma'am

lilly: I think they are getting rosier

Constance Pennington Smythe: Very good. So what do you do when you are alone?

lilly: oh i dress in something comfortable and then i watch some sissy training videos; of course i am locked up so i won't be a bad girl

Constance Pennington Smythe: Very nice. You should also practice walking in heels.

lilly: i was practicing my walk earlier

Constance Pennington Smythe: Do you read magazines like Vogue, In Style, or Harpers Bazaar?

lilly: When i find them available like at a doctors office or dentist

Constance Pennington Smythe: Your Wife/or Mistress doesn't have them around the house?

lilly: no

Constance Pennington Smythe: Yes, I hope you're not "too" comfortable when you said you like to dress comfortable. Do you own a girdle? I love to put my girls in severe girdles.

lilly: Yes Ma'am and a corset but just a panty girdle

lilly: now i just have pink satin panties on

Constance Pennington Smythe: Hmm, I'd like to see you in a long-line, very tight, open-bottom girdle. I prefer those so my friends and guests (male and female) can grope my girls at will. You do understand that you will be available for everyone's pleasure and amusement?

lilly: Oh yes Ma'am, how divine that would be

lilly: i shall try to acquire one in the near future

Constance Pennington Smythe: Yes, baby, when

some large male hand paws your balls you're to swoon and bat your eyelashes to show HIM how much you appreciate the attention.

lilly: oh yes Ma'am and look up at him always

Constance Pennington Smythe: Of course! And when one of my Female friends wants to introduce their niece to the art of plugging a sissy bottom you're to smile - bend over - and offer it up.

lilly: of course Ma'am that would be my pleasure and well as please your Female friends also

Constance Pennington Smythe: And sweetheart, it's OK for 'you' to enjoy it as well. That's how sissies get their pleasure. Pinch the nipples again, baby, keep pinching them for me.

lilly: my nipple a quite sore as i have been taking herbs and i think i might be developing something under my nipples Ma'am, but i will continue to pinch them

Constance Pennington Smythe: Then don't be too hard on them, maybe lightly stroke them.

lilly: Yes Ma'am that feels better

Constance Pennington Smythe: Are you leaking at all dear? Any pre-sissy-cream?

lilly: Oh yes Ma'am a lot

Constance Pennington Smythe: Wipe it up and recycle baby, lick it up. My Lady friends LOVE to watch sissies recycle.

lilly: as a matter of fact its in a small dish

Constance Pennington Smythe: Maybe rub a bit on your nipples, that would be soooo sexy.

lilly: oh yes ma'am

Constance Pennington Smythe: Can you leave it there? All night? Sleep with sissy cream that I milked from you on your nipples?

lilly: i have enough for a small salad <giggles>

lilly: Yes Ma'am i will do that

Constance Pennington Smythe: Oh baby, would that be 'deliciously' evil. I'd take you to dinner and order you a salad and tell the waiter to hold your dressing, we have our own 'special' blend.

lilly: Oh yes Ma'am that would be very special

Constance Pennington Smythe: And under your trousers you'd have a garter belt and stockings, and a plug up that sissi pussi.

lilly: oooh that makes me squirm Ma'am

lilly: i was plugged and chaste last night

Constance Pennington Smythe: Under that dress shirt we'd have you in a light, wispy bra, the cups filled with steel wool.

lilly: ouch my nipples would be so sore

Constance Pennington Smythe: But you'd sit through dinner - and suffer - for me, wouldn't you?

lilly: i would have to keep them covered with special cream. Oh, of course I would Mistress with a smile

Constance Pennington Smythe: How much cream could I milk from you - I wonder? At first you might even enjoy it. But then - then you'd beg me to stop, crawl to me and beg me not to make you cum. Sorry baby, I want more. You've got 5 minutes to fill this shot glass or you'll be whipped - on that sissy clitty you seem to love so much. Cum for me - NOW.

lilly: Yes Ma'am I have most of a shot glass already

Constance Pennington Smythe: I'm claiming those balls, and I'll have what's in them - ALL OF IT.

lilly: Yes Ma'am everything in them belongs to you to do with as you desire<curtsey>

Constance Pennington Smythe: Then empty them baby, in honor of me. I want you to give yourself a cum facial.

lilly: OH Ma'am they are pretty empty now, but not a whole shot glass full i'm sorry to say

Constance Pennington Smythe: Let's be sure. Do I have to slip on a latex glove and milk that ass?

lilly: Ma'am i'm sure they are pretty dry

Constance Pennington Smythe: Good girl, such a wanton little slut you are. So fun to play with.

lilly: do you think my face needs some repair

Constance Pennington Smythe: Yes, rub some of that cum on there. I mean, it's not the same thing as kneeling before Master Alex and feeling those thick streams of real man cum coat your face, but we'll work with what we have - for now.

lilly: any place in particular?

Constance Pennington Smythe: Around the nose and lips. I want you to smell it - to taste it. Get used to it.

lilly: yes Ma'am i have it all over those areas now

Constance Pennington Smythe: Good, now stick out your tongue and see what you can lick off. It will be good practice: 1. In getting used to the taste and 2: Getting that tongue nice and limber to lick a Lady's bottom.

lilly: Yes Ma'am are there any other place i should rub it

Constance Pennington Smythe: Rub what you have left over your titties. Of course someday we will get you those massive 44FF globes and you'll NEVER be able to produce enough cum for those, but for now rub it on your sissy titties.

lilly: i have more than enough for my little titties

Constance Pennington Smythe: Is it sticky? Don't wash your hands, lick it off. Clean your hands with your lips and tongue, some of a sissy's favorite tools.

lilly: yes Ma'am i will do that

lilly: there still more Ma'am

Constance Pennington Smythe: More? Goodness. Wipe some on that sissy clitty. Does it feel good? fondling yourself? Imagine my friends and I watching you, laughing.

lilly: But im in a cb3000 Ma'am

Constance Pennington Smythe: Wipe it on your balls, those useless male balls. Hold them in your hands and know that WE control you through the balls.

lilly: yes Maam

Constance Pennington Smythe: You've been a VERY good slut this evening. Mistress is pleased with the way you've entertained me. I'm going to relax with a Cognac before bed. Have a good evening.

lilly: thank you so very much for Your time Ma'am if i may assist you in any way please let me know. I hope you have wonderful brandy dreams

Constance Pennington Smythe: Keep checking in baby. We'll hook up. XOXO

lilly: thank you <curtsey>

lilly: good night Ma'am

*****

prissy maid: Good evening Mistress Constance, prissy maid: how are You today?

Constance Pennington Smythe: Hello, baby. Are you properly dressed to talk to me?

prissy maid: Yes Mistress, i am. i am wearing one of my gray maids service uniforms, Mistress.

Constance Pennington Smythe: Lovely. My petal has a black/white and a blue pinstripe with white accent housekeeping uniforms. I actually purchased them from an actual domestic uniform site on the web. That flouncy, silky French Maid fluff is fine for show...but "I" expect a fully-functioning WORKING maid - not a decoration.

prissy maid: Yes Mistress, that is how Mistress feels also. Mistress has a series of maids service dresses for me to wear that are for daily sissy maid duty. The frilly sissy maids dress are for scenes, special days, etc., Mistress.

Constance Pennington Smythe: Very nice - and you're wearing heels? Details, sweetheart.

prissy maid: Yes Mistress, not very high ones, today Mistress, they are 2.5 inch , working heels, Mistress, calls them. Black. Mistress. i also have on a white tea apron, Mistress.

prissy maid: i have been on service call for Mistress today, as She was home today, Mistress.

Constance Pennington Smythe: Yes, petal also has some more substantial heels for 'working.'

Constance Pennington Smythe: Are you wearing stockings, pantyhose or tights? What does your Mistress prefer?

prissy maid: i am sorry Mistress, i meant to

include those details, please forgive me, yes Mistress, i wear thigh highs most days, in a service uniform Mistress. For the gray dress, either nude, black, or gray in color, Mistress.

Constance Pennington Smythe: petal also has an assortment of legwear, as well as some cute lacy ankle socks that look darling with stilettos.

prissy maid: Mistress has me wear little lacy ankle socks at times, Mistress.

Constance Pennington Smythe: I autographed a book to you and sent it on to my publisher with two of petal's special Delrin canes. You ought to have it - next week? I'll be on a business trip all week, without my laptop, it can be such a hassle at times.

prissy maid: Thank You so much Mistress, it is so special to me to have something that special from You.

Constance Pennington Smythe: You're welcome sweetheart, but I expect that your Mistress will make you suffer with those canes - at least I hope so. Oh, to see you flinch, to see the red welts, hear your squeals.

prissy maid: Yes Mistress, thank You so much Mistress. Mistress has plans for something special in a scene with Your canes Mistress.

Constance Pennington Smythe: I'd LOVE to see a picture of your welted ass, the white creamy skin, striped red.

prissy maid: Mistress may put up some pictures also along with some others She would like to put on on of the sites, Mistress.

Constance Pennington Smythe: i'm thinking of getting a little school girl outfit for petal: white blouse, mini-mini-plaid skirt, knee-highs, heels.

prissy maid: Oh yes Mistress! That would be so neat for petal to wear, Mistress.

prissy maid: Will You be having school with petal, Mistress?

Constance Pennington Smythe: MMM, a naughty school girl? Bent over the desk and caned?

prissy maid: Yes Mistress, a full school scene with petal, i can see You with petal in that kind of training for petal, Mistress.

Constance Pennington Smythe: During a visit to Las Vegas we went to The Luxor for a day. I bought petal a belly dance skirt and one of the beaded headpieces. When we got home I made him buy some beginning bellydance DVDs. Soon he will put on a show for me.

prissy maid: Yes Mistress, Mistress has been talking to me about expanding my dancing, as You know Mistress, i have ballet lessons with Mistress each week, Mistress.

Constance Pennington Smythe: Remind me again, baby, are you in chastity? Surely your Mistress doesn't have a use for that thing other than an amusement or something to torment you.

prissy maid: Yes Mistress, i am in chastity 24/7. Mistress. Mistress has me under the strictest of control and rules, Mistress.

prissy maid: yes Mistress, i am sorry i am slow tonight, thank You Mistress.

prissy maid: And yes Mistress to the torment part of Your chastity question, Mistress.

Constance Pennington Smythe: Sometimes I make petal kneel by my bed while I take my pleasure in any number of ways. Then he is dismissed and crawls, frustrated, down the hall to his maid's room. He was long ago banished from Mistress's suite. Alone in his room he'll try and achieve 'some' pleasure from his nipples and pussi.

prissy maid: Yes Mistress, i do understand about Your training of petal. Mistress pleasures Herself regularly while i am allowed no relief, etc. Mistress. i am on call, as She does this, Mistress.

prissy maid: i am not allowed to touch my sissy nipples without orders, Mistress.

Constance Pennington Smythe: My, that 'is' strict.

prissy maid: Yes Mistress, thank You Mistress.

prissy maid: Mistress has ordered me to inform You Mistress, that i must keep a daily record sheet with any infractions, such as clitty reactions, nipple touching, etc. all of which, is not allowed Mistress.

Constance Pennington Smythe: Really? I do applaud such record keeping. At the end of the week is the list tabulated? Are you punished for infractions?

prissy maid: Yes Mistress, that is exactly what Mistress does each week Mistress, Mistress counts up each item and translates that into Her punishment and discipline scenes with me Mistress.

prissy maid: Mistress has a system for infraction count, Mistress.

Constance Pennington Smythe: One VERY effective punishment for petal is to deny him his feminine clothes, keep him naked. he SO loves his dresses, high heels and earrings. he'd MUCH rather take a caning than be denied his precious stilettos!

prissy maid: Oh Yes Mistress! i do understand how petal feels Mistress. Mistress makes me earn my frillies for wearing each week, Mistress. So i do understand how petal feels Mistress.

Constance Pennington Smythe: Are you ever exhibited before others?

prissy maid: Yes Mistress. Mistress has other Dominant friends Mistress. They have their submissivies, so Yes Mistress, i am, Mistress.

Constance Pennington Smythe: Do you like that? The public humiliation? I think you do.

prissy maid: Yes Mistress, i do like it Mistress. Thank You for asking Mistress.

Constance Pennington Smythe: Good for you and your Mistress, baby!

prissy maid: Thank You Mistress, You are so kind Mistress. i love to talk to You Mistress. i have the highest respect for You Mistress.

Constance Pennington Smythe: Thank you, darling. And we respect our submissives, even as we abuse and humiliate them.

prissy maid: Oh Yes Mistress! All that and more, i do love to suffer and serve Mistress and You, Mistress. Thank You Mistress!

Constance Pennington Smythe: I have to sign off now, baby. If we don't hook up before I leave this weekend we'll hook up when I get back. Give my regards to your Mistress.

prissy maid: Yes Mistress, thank You for tonight Mistress, i will miss You Mistress and think of You Mistress. Mistress sends Her regards also Mistress. Have a nice trip Mistress, good night Mistress.

Constance Pennington Smythe: XOXO

*****

sissy pammy: good evening Mistress...

Constance Pennington Smythe: Hello, darling. Are you dressed properly to chat with me? Details, sweetie.

sissy pammy: fishnets, thong lycra panties, bra, corset, fishnet gloves, 5" heels and leather bondage cuffs/collar Mistress

Constance Pennington Smythe: Mmmm, are you left alone? Mistress out for the evening?

sissy pammy: she's in another part of the house Mistress

sissy pammy: doesn't know i'm online right now

Constance Pennington Smythe: Do you have permission to 'play' with others? Not sneaking around behind HER back are we? THAT would be wrong.

sissy pammy: i sort of have permission Mistress

Constance Pennington Smythe: Hmmm, and you'll 'sort of' get caned if you fuck up?

sissy pammy: well, yes Mistress

Constance Pennington Smythe: Does your Mistress discipline you?

sissy pammy: usually not with physical punishment Mistress

Constance Pennington Smythe: Pity, I dearly love to stripe a pristine sissy ass.

Constance Pennington Smythe: Have you printed out my Femdom 101 guide for your Mistress? It's on my web site.

sissy pammy: no Mistress, but i will

sissy pammy: i've also looked at your recent homework assignments, and will submit mine in the near future

Constance Pennington Smythe: Very good. Your past assignments have been very nice. I have hundreds of members. Can you imagine them all looking at your assignments?

sissy pammy: *gets excited at the thought, but the cage controls that option*

Constance Pennington Smythe: Does your Mistress hold the key?

sissy pammy: yes Mistress

Constance Pennington Smythe: I hold petal's key. But "I" get all the sex I want, while he is denied.

Constance Pennington Smythe: Do you service your Mistress so she is afforded all pleasures?

sissy pammy: yes Mistress

sissy pammy: sorry, need to run Mistress

Constance Pennington Smythe: Later, slut. XOXO

*****

sissy "o": How are You?

Constance Pennington Smythe: Hello, darling. Are you dressed properly to chat with me? Details, darling.

sissy "o": Yes, but not too sexy though

Constance Pennington Smythe: I'll decide what is sexy.

sissy "o": A simple black satin teddy for bed, pink panties.

Constance Pennington Smythe: Remove the panties. I may want access to those items before we're finished here.

sissy "o": Yes, but i am a bit shocked.

Constance Pennington Smythe: Get over it - and get the panties off. Slip on some heels as well; I like my 'girls' in heels.

sissy "o": Ok, give me a few minutes, i need to go upstairs.

sissy "o": i feel very weird dressed this way

sissy "o": or should i say undressed

Constance Pennington Smythe: It's not about what you want, sweetheart. It's about what "I" want: a high-heeled, pantyless slut in a black nightie. And I have what I want now. Pinch those nipples for me; make them perky.

sissy "o": Yes, they are now perky, Ms.

Constance Pennington Smythe: Good. About your 'clitty' and those balls, dear. Are they shaved? Do you keep it shaved and moisturized down there?

sissy "o": shaved but not always moisturized, not really thought about it.

Constance Pennington Smythe: You need to start moisturizing down there. Visit a drug store and buy some lotion, preferably something with vitamin E and Collagen, if you can find it. "IF" I ever decide to touch you there (wouldn't you LOVE that!) I want it to be smooth to my touch.

sissy "o": Would regular moisturizing creme do? It would be such an honor if Ms deems to touch Your sissy. i do use moisturizing wash so i guess i am pretty smooth.

Constance Pennington Smythe: Yes, darling, anything would be preferable to not moisturizing. Of course you'd be restrained while I touched you. Maybe even gagged so all I'd hear are sissy moans.

Constance Pennington Smythe: Perhaps I'd restrain you on a bondage table, or over a spanking horse.

sissy "o": Either way i will be so weak on my knees and breathing heavily, tormented by my omnipotent Ms present.

Constance Pennington Smythe: I can see your eyes grow wide as I slowly slip on my elbow-length leather gloves. Over them, petal pulls on latex gloves and then lubes my fingers. When I bend down my hair brushes your chest; you catch the scent of my Chanel perfume.

sissy "o": Ms, i think i am losing my senses.

Constance Pennington Smythe: petal gently takes your clitty between his lips while my finger probes your puckered opening. Oh! You flinched, but that's why we restrained you. Relax and breathe sweetheart.

sissy "o": My moans would be all muffled, i would be shaking by now. i wish i can breath normally but it is beyond this sissy's control.

Constance Pennington Smythe: I like the way your eyelids fluttered when I slipped one finger in. Let's try two - shall we? "petal, gently suck sissy "o"'s clitty, but don't make her cum. We'll see how long we can tease her." (I wiggle my finger and you moan). "Mmm, what have I found here?"

sissy "o": Mmmm, can't speak. What did You find Ms?

Constance Pennington Smythe: Your little prosty

nubbin. Let me play with it while my other leather gloved hand finds one of your nipples. Oh, I love the confusion on your face: the glorious bliss of me milking you and the pain as my finger pinches your nipple. It's all running together isn't it. "petal, flick your tongue over the head of her sissy clitty."

sissy "o": Ms, i think that at this time my sissy mind would have imagined that i have died and gone to sissy heaven.

Constance Pennington Smythe: I'm going to milk you, baby, pump that sissy goo right out of you and into petal's mouth. Give it up baby, let it go. Can you feel me massaging you inside? Mmm, feels good, doesn't it. Squirt for Mistress, fill my sissy's mouth with your sissy cream. If you don't do it now, I'm locking it away - who knows when you'll get another chance?

sissy "o": Ms, no sissy can stand this. i think i will have lost it already.

Constance Pennington Smythe: Squirt for me. "petal, hold all that sissy cream in your mouth. Then we'll take off her gag and you two can share a sissy kiss."

sissy "o": Yes, sissy "o" would be so grateful.

Constance Pennington Smythe: Yes, I suppose I do spoil my sluts.

sissy "o": So what should sissy "o" do to repay Ms supreme kindness after this?

Constance Pennington Smythe: I want you to cum for me, rub it on your nipples and sleep with it on there. Maybe we'll hook up later this weekend and you can tell me how it all made you feel.

sissy "o": What about in the scene, should sissy pay homage to Ms?

Constance Pennington Smythe: Darling, I'm not staying around for that. After I've had my fun with you I'll go upstairs to enjoy a glass of wine. petal will release you, get you cleaned up, and then you will both crawl upstairs to worship the soles of my high heels.

sissy "o": Yes, i guess my sissy eyes would be consumed by tears of gratefulness and worship while licking Your heels.

Constance Pennington Smythe: "IF" I'm feeling 'too' generous I may let you and petal sleep together, although you'll both be securely locked in chastity devices. If you can find other means of pleasing each other...

sissy "o": i am already milked, i guess i am ok but poor petal might be having trouble sleeping.

Constance Pennington Smythe: You two can suck each other's nipples, probe the bumholes with your fingers. Maybe I'll give you each a spritz of perfume, so you smell pretty.

sissy "o": Oh You are so kind. petal will be in heaven with my C-cup.

Constance Pennington Smythe: Sissies playing with nipples - heaven.

sissy "o": Ms, Your sissy "o" is a shemale with 36C-26-36 figure. And she is all yours to use and abuse, and of course to obey.

Constance Pennington Smythe: Goodness, Master will love you.

sissy "o": Yes, what would he want to do to sissy "o"?

Constance Pennington Smythe: He'd want to see you on your knees, those 36C titties heaving with the excitement of seeing his Alpha Male cock.

sissy "o": Yes, Ms. sissy "o" is maid to please.

Constance Pennington Smythe: That's the convenience of a sissy maid. I mean - we know that real men love blow jobs, but I'm not going there, sweetheart. Not when I have sissy maids.

sissy "o": Yes, Ma'am. sissy "o" would be the best fluff girl for You.

Constance Pennington Smythe: That's the convenience I offer my male guests and visitors - unlimited blow jobs. You want sucked off 10 times a day? Simply ring that crystal bell - here comes sissy "o". Isn't she pretty? On your knees girl.

sissy "o": 10 times a day. i guess sissy "o" will have sore jaw after that.

Constance Pennington Smythe: But Master will be pleased, you do want to please him don't you? When he picks me up for a date and loves the way I look and gets excited; we can't mess up my makeup and hair. That's why I have a sissy maid to assuage those male needs, while I stay pretty and perfectly coiffed.

sissy "o": Of course, sissy will be glad that she can be of service to Mistress & Master.

Constance Pennington Smythe: Maybe, if you're a good girl, you can lick and suck Master's balls while he makes love to me.

sissy "o": Does sissy get to orally please Ms also?

Constance Pennington Smythe: Maybe, but only AFTER it's been used. Clean pussies aren't for sissies, only used ones, full of real man spunk.

sissy "o": sissy will definitely make sure that Mistress's feminine shrine is well cleansed. sissy was told that "sissy don't get pussy, she is a pussy". sissy will treasure this opportunity.

Constance Pennington Smythe: We'll want Master's cock licked clean as well. Who knows, you may get him to rise to the occasion again.

sissy "o": Well sissy definitely will not disappoint. sissy will make sure Mistress & Master are well attended, knowing that her pierced clitty will only be unlocked when Mistress is well satisfied.

Constance Pennington Smythe: I'm glad you know your place. It's after midnight, sweetheart, time for Mistress to retire.

sissy "o": Thanks Ms for training me. Good night.

Constance Pennington Smythe: XOXO

sissy "o": This is definitely the hottest chat i have so far. Bye.

Constance Pennington Smythe: You're sweet, baby. Such a good girl.

END